RITUAL IN DEATH AND MISSING IN DEATH

J. D. ROBB

LARGE PRINT

Oxford

First published in Great Britain 2013
by
Piatkus
an imprint of Little, Brown Book Group

Published in Large Print 2015 by ISIS Publishing Ltd.,
7 Centremead, Osney Mead, Oxford OX2 0ES
by arrangement with
Little, Brown Book Group
an Hachette UK Company

CIP data is available for this title from the British Library

ISBN 978–1–4450–9910–1 (hb)
ISBN 978–1–4450–9911–8 (pb)

Printed and bound in Great Britain by
T. J. International Ltd., Padstow, Cornwall

RITUAL IN DEATH
AND
MISSING IN DEATH

RITUAL IN DEATH

One owes respect to the living; to the dead one owes only the truth.

VOLTAIRE

The belief in a supernatural source of evil is not necessary; men alone are quite capable of every wickedness.

JOSEPH CONRAD

CHAPTER
ONE

Her feet were killing her. And made her imagine traveling back in time, hunting down whoever had invented stiletto heels, and beating the crap out of him.

What was the point of them other than throwing a woman off balance, making it next to impossible to run, and inducing foot cramps?

The question occupied Eve's mind as she tuned out the bulk of the party conversation buzzing around her like a hive of drunk hornets. What if one of the guests at this shindig went off and . . . stabbed somebody in the eye with a shrimp fork, for instance? How was she supposed to take him down dressed like this? And a foot pursuit in these stilts? Forget about it.

It was a hell of a get-up for a cop, to her way of thinking. The flimsy excuse for a dress left most of her exposed. And she glittered. You couldn't have diamonds hanging all over you and blend.

Of course, you couldn't go to any sort of snazzy function with Roarke and blend.

The only advantage to the ridiculous damn shoes that she could see was the fact that they boosted her up so that she and Roarke were eye-to-eye.

They were stupendous eyes, bold and brilliantly blue. A look from them could give her a tingle in the belly — even after nearly two years of marriage. The rest of him didn't suck either, she reflected. The black silk fall of hair framed a billion-dollar jackpot of a face. Even now, as he glanced at her, that sculpted, delicious mouth curved up in a slow, secret smile.

All she had to do, Eve reminded herself, was tolerate the goddamn shoes a couple more hours, then she'd have that mouth — and the rest of the package — to herself. Screaming arches were probably a small price to pay.

"Darling." Roarke took a glass of champagne from the waiter passing them, and handed it to her. Since the glass he'd traded it for had still been half full, she interpreted it as a signal to tune back in.

Okay, okay, she thought. She was here as Roarke's spouse. It wasn't as if he demanded she gear up like this and attend excruciatingly boring parties every day of the week. He was smooth about it — and as the man had more money than God and nearly as much power and position — the least she could do was play the part when they were doing the public couple thing.

Their hostess, one Maxia Carlyle, glided over in some kind of floaty number. The wealthy socialite was — by her own words — kicking into New York for a few days to catch up with friends. All of whom, Eve supposed, were wandering around Maxia's expansive tri-level hotel suite gorging on canapés and sloshing down champagne.

"I haven't had a minute to talk to you." Maxia put her hand on Roarke's arm, tipped her face to his.

They looked, Eve decided, like an ad for the rich and the gorgeous.

"And how've you been, Maxi?"

"Oh, you know how it goes." She laughed, shrugging one perfect bare shoulder. "It's been about four years, hasn't it, since we've seen each other. Never seem to land in the same place at the same time, so I'm especially glad you could make it tonight. And you," she added with a sparkling smile for Eve. "I was hoping I'd get the chance to meet you. Roarke's cop."

"Mostly the NYPSD considers me theirs."

"I can't even imagine it. What it must be like. Your work must be so fascinating and exciting. Investigating murders and murderers."

"It has its moments."

"More than moments, I'm sure. I've seen you on screen from time to time. The Icove case in particular."

And wasn't that one going to dog her forever? Eve mused.

"I have to say you don't look anything like a policewoman." Maxia's perfect eyebrows arched as she gave Eve's dress a quick scan. "Leonardo dresses you, doesn't he?"

"No, I usually do it myself."

Roarke gave her a little elbow poke. "Eve's oldest friend is married to Leonardo. Eve often wears him."

"Mavis Freestone is your oldest friend?" Now, in addition to interest and curiosity, considerable warmth infused Maxia's face. "I love her music, but my niece is a slathering fan. I took her to one of Mavis's concerts, in London, and arranged for a backstage pass. She was so sweet with my niece, and I've been the undisputed champion of aunts ever since."

She laughed, touched Eve's arm. "You *do* have a fascinating life. Married to Roarke, friends with Mavis and Leonardo, and chasing killers. I suppose it's mostly head work, isn't it? Studying evidence, looking for clues. People like me glamorize it, think about police work the way it is on screen and at the vids. All danger and action, chasing madmen down dark alleys and firing off your weapon, when in reality it's brain and paperwork."

"Yeah." Eve controlled the urge to smirk. "That's about it."

"Being married to Roarke's action enough. Are you still dangerous?" Maxia asked him.

"Domesticated." He lifted Eve's hand, kissed it. "Entirely."

"I don't believe that for a minute. Oh, there's Anton. I need to snatch him away and bring him over to meet you."

Eve took a long, long drink of champagne.

"We'll meet this Anton, mingle another twenty," Roarke said, the faint hint of Ireland in his voice, "and slip out and away."

Eve felt a tingle of joy, right down to her numbed toes. "Seriously?"

"I never intended to stay above an hour or so. And certainly owe you for the points I'm making by bringing a Homicide cop to the party."

"It's all paperwork," Eve said dryly.

He skimmed a finger down her arm, where a knife had slashed only days before. "Yes, your work is nothing but tedium. But I have to agree with Maxi. You don't look very coplike tonight."

"Good thing I don't have to chase down any psycho killers. I'd fall off these stupid shoes and embarrass myself." She curled her toes in them — or attempted to while she flicked a hand at the short, choppy crop of brown hair she'd recently taken the scissors to herself. Old priceless diamonds dripped from her ears. "I don't get parties like this. People standing around. Talk, talk, talk. Why do they have to get all dressed up to do that?"

"To show off."

She thought about that over another sip of wine. "I guess that's it. At least I don't have to gear up like this for the shower deal for Louise. Still, another party. More talk, talk, talk."

"It's a ritual, after all. When a friend's about to marry, her friends gather together, with gifts, and . . . well, I have no idea what happens then."

"If it's anything like mine, some of them drink till they puke, and others strip it off and dance."

"Sorry I'll miss it."

"Liar." But she grinned at him.

"Here we are!" Maxia came back, towing a portly, mustachioed man somewhere on the shady side of sixty. On his arm like a whippy vine twined a woman well shy of thirty with full, pouty lips, a bored expression, and a short red dress that covered very little of her expansive breasts.

"You simply must meet Anton and his lovely companion. It's Satin, isn't it?"

"Silk," the bored blonde corrected.

"Of course it is."

Eve caught the quick glint in Maxia's eyes and understood she'd *mistaken* the name deliberately. And liked her better for it.

"Actually we met a few years ago." Anton stuck out a wide, pudgy hand. "At Wimbledon."

"It's nice to see you again. My wife, Eve."

"Yes, the American cop. A pleasure, Detective."

"Lieutenant." Eve glanced down at Silk's sky-high heels. Just heels, she noted, with the feet arched into them bare on top. "I heard about those." She pointed. "People are actually wearing invisible shoes."

"They're not available to the public for another three weeks." Silk tossed her long mane of hair. "Sookie pulled some strings." She plastered herself against Anton/Sookie.

"Anton's produced several films about crime and police and so on," Maxia commented. "So I thought he'd enjoy meeting one of New York's Finest."

"British-style procedurals." Anton patted Silk's hand as she tugged at him like a petulant child. "What we like to think of as crackling whodunits — with plenty of sex and violence," he added with a laugh. "And a slight connection with reality, as you'd know. I have been thinking about using an American setting, so I —"

"I don't see why a girl would want to be a cop." Silk frowned at Eve. "It's not very feminine."

"Really? It's funny because I don't see why a *girl* would want to be a bimb —"

"What is it you do?" Roarke cut Eve off, smoothly — giving her only the slightest pinch on the ass.

"I'm an actress. I just finished shooting a major role in Sookie's next vid."

"Victim, right?" Eve asked.

"I get to die dramatically. It's going to make me a star, isn't it, Sookie?"

"Absolutely, sweetheart."

"I want to go. There's nothing happening here. I want to go dancing, go some place with some *action*." She tugged hard enough to pull Anton back a few steps.

"He used to be such a sensible man," Maxia murmured.

"Guys of a certain age are especially vulnerable to bimboitis."

Maxia laughed. "I'm so glad I like you. I wish I wasn't due in Prague in a couple of days so I could get to know you better. I should mingle, make sure everyone isn't as bored as Linen over there."

"I think that's Polyester. Definitely man-made fibers."

Laughing again, Maxia shook her head. "Yes, I really like you. And you." She rose to her toes to kiss Roarke's cheek. "You look awfully happy."

"I am. And awfully glad to see you again, Maxi."

As Maxia started to turn, Silk's strident voice whined out. "But I want to go *now*. I want to have *fun*. This party is *dead*."

Someone screamed. Something crashed. As people stumbled back, as some turned, shoving through small packs of others, Eve pushed forward.

The man staggered like a drunk, and wore nothing but spatters and smears of blood. The knife clutched in his hand gleamed with it.

A woman in his path fainted, and managed to take out a waiter holding a full tray of canapés with her. As shrimp balls and quail eggs rained, Silk shrieked, turned, and in a sprint for the terrace bowled over guests like pins in an alley.

Eve flipped open the next-to-useless bag she carried, tossed it to Roarke as she pulled out her weapon.

"Drop it. Drop it now." She sized him up quickly. About five feet ten inches, roughly one-sixty-five. Caucasian, brown and brown. And the brown eyes were glazed and glassy. Shock or drugs — maybe both.

"Drop it," she repeated when he took another staggering step forward. "Or I drop you."

"What?" His gaze skidded around the room. "What? What is it?"

She considered and rejected just stunning him in a matter of seconds. Instead she moved to him, gripped the wrist of his knife hand, twisted. "Drop the goddamn knife."

His eyes stared into hers as his fingers went limp. She heard the knife hit the floor. "Nobody touch it. Stay back. I'm the police, do you get that? I'm a cop. What are you on?"

"I don't know. I don't know. The police? Can you help me? I think I killed someone. Can you help me?"

12

"Yeah. You bet. Roarke, I need a field kit ASAP, and for you to call this in. I need everyone else upstairs for now. I need you people to clear this room until the situation is contained. Move it!" she snapped when people stood, gaping. "And somebody check on that woman lying in the shrimp balls over there."

Roarke stepped up beside her. "I've sent one of the hotel staff down to the garage to get the field kit out of the boot of the car," he told her. "I've notified your Dispatch."

"Thanks." She stood where she was as the naked party crasher sat on the floor and began to shudder. "Just remember, you're the one who wanted to come tonight."

With a nod, Roarke planted a foot on the hilt of the knife to secure it. "No one to blame but myself."

"Can you get my recorder out of that stupid purse?"

"You brought a recorder?"

"If you need the weapon, you're going to need the recorder."

When he handed it to her, Eve pinned it to the frothy material over her breasts, engaged it. After reciting the basics, she crouched down. "Who do you think you killed?"

"I don't know."

"What's your name?"

"It's . . ." He lifted a blood-smeared hand, rubbed it over his face. "I can't think. I can't remember. I can't think."

"Tell me what you took."

"Took?"

"Drugs. Illegals."

"I . . . I don't do illegals. Do I? There's so much blood." He lifted his hands, stared at them. "Do you see all this blood?"

"Yeah." She looked up at Roarke. "It's fresh. I'm going to need to do a room-to-room, starting with this floor. He couldn't have walked around for long like this. We start with this floor."

"I can arrange that. Do you want security to start on that, or sit on him while you do the room-to-room?"

"Sit on him. I don't want them to talk to him, touch him. What's that room over there?"

"It would be a maid's room."

"That'll do."

"Eve," Roarke said as she straightened. "I don't see any wounds on him. If that blood's someone else's — that much blood — they can't possibly still be alive."

"No, but we push the room-to-room first."

CHAPTER
TWO

She needed to move fast. The amount of blood on her naked guy made it doubtful she'd find anyone alive — if she found anyone at all — so she couldn't putz around. While she didn't much like leaving her suspect with hotel security, even once she'd clapped on the restraints from her field kit, she couldn't afford to wait for her uniformed backup, or her partner.

For lack of better, she set her suspect on the floor of the maid's room, ran his prints.

"Jackson Pike." She crouched down on his level, looked into the glazed brown eyes. "Jack?"

"What?"

"What happened, Jack?"

"I don't . . ." He looked around the room, dazed and stoned. "I don't . . ." Then he moaned in pain and clutched his head.

"Uniformed officers are on their way," she said to the pair from security as she straightened. "I want him exactly where I've left him, and those people upstairs contained until I get back. Nobody comes in except NYPSD officials. Nobody goes out. Let's move," she said to Roarke.

"Guy's a doctor," she continued as they started out the door. "Thirty-three years old. Single."

"He didn't walk in off the street like that."

"No. Your hotel. Find out if a Jackson Pike, or anyone with a variation of that name's registered. How's this floor set up?"

Roarke pulled out his 'link as he gestured. "Four triplexes, one on each corner. One minute."

While he spoke to the hotel manager, Eve turned left. "Well, he left a trail. That's handy." Moving quickly, she followed bloody footprints over the lush carpet.

"No Jackson Pike, or any Pikes for that matter," Roarke told her. "There's a Jackson, Carl, on thirty-two. They're checking. On this floor Maxia has 600. Six-oh-two is occupied by Domingo Fellini — actor — I saw him at the party."

"Pike didn't come from there, trail's down this way." She picked up the pace as they started down the long corridor. "It's the sixtieth floor. Why isn't it 6002?"

"The sixth floor is the health club, the pool, and so on. No guest rooms. The triplexes cater to those who can afford the freight, and we bill them as penthouses, or apartments. So it's Suite 600. Perception."

"Yeah, your perception's pretty screwed with all this blood on your carpet. Anyone in 604?"

"Not tonight."

"Empty suite's a nice spot for bloody murder, but the trail heads off." She kept moving, her weapon in her hand, her eyes scanning. "Does every suite have the private elevator like Suite 600?"

16

"They do, yes. Those elevators in the center of the floor are also private, in that you need a key card or clearance for the trip up."

Emergency exits, all four corners, she noted, via stairs. But Jackson Pike hadn't used them. His trail led straight to the carved double doors of Suite 606.

Eve saw the faint smear of blood over the ornate zero.

Suite 666, she thought. Wasn't that just perfect?

She signaled for Roarke to stay back, then tried the knob.

"Locked. I don't have my master."

"Lucky for you, you have me." He drew a slim tool out of his pocket.

"Handy, but have you ever considered how a cop's supposed to explain — should it come up — why her husband's got burglary tools in his pockets?"

"For bloody emergencies?" He straightened. "Lock's off."

"I don't suppose you're carrying."

He flicked her a look, his eyes very cool. "While I didn't think it necessary to bring a weapon to a cocktail party, I got this from security." He drew out a stunner. "Civilian issue. Perfectly legal."

"Hmm. On three."

It wasn't their first time through a door. She went low, he went high into a large living area lit by hundreds of candles. In the flickering light blood gleamed as it pooled over the black pentagram drawn on the polished marble floor.

17

A body floated on that pool, the arms and legs spread to form an X at the center of the sign.

Gone, Eve thought, bled out. Throat slashed, multiple body wounds. She shook her head at Roarke, gestured to the left.

She moved right, in a suite the mirror image of Maxia's. Sweeping her weapon, she cleared a dining room, a short hallway, a kitchen, a powder room, making the circle that brought her back to Roarke.

"Bed and bath clear, this level," he told her. "Both were used. There's considerable blood — smears not spatters. Hers, I expect."

He wasn't a cop, she mused, but he could think like one. "We're going up." She did a chin point toward the elevator and tried to ignore the stench — not just death, but a kind of burning on the air. "Can you block that? Shut it down?"

Saying nothing, he walked to it, took out his tool again. While he worked, Eve circled the pentagram to clear the terrace.

"Done."

"What's the layout on the second floor?"

"Bed and bath, small sitting room to the left. Master suite — living area, powder room, dressing area, bed and bath to the right."

"I'll take the right."

The place felt empty, she thought. It felt dead. The metallic reek of the blood, the sickly sweet overlay of death mixed with candle wax smeared the air. And something more, that burning and a kind of . . .

pulsing, she thought. Spent energy, the shadows of it still beating.

Together they cleared the second level, then the third.

She found evidence of sexual frenzy, of food, of drink, of murder. "The sweepers are going to be hours in here, if not days."

Roarke studied the glasses, plates, half-eaten food. "What kind of people do murder, and leave so much of themselves behind?"

"The kind who think they're beyond or above the law. The worst kind. I need to seal this place off, all three levels, until crime scene gets here. Who was registered in this suite?"

"The Asant Group." On the steps, he stared down at the body posed on the pentagram. "Jumble the letters, and you've got —"

"Satan. God, I hate this kind of shit. People want to worship the devil, be my guest. Hell, they can have horns surgically implanted on their forehead. But then they've just got to slice somebody up for their human sacrifice and drag me into it."

"Damned cheeky of them."

"I'll say."

"Naked Jack didn't do this on his own."

"Nope. Let's go see if his memory's a little clearer."

The uniforms had taken over. Eve directed them to take names and contact info from the guests, then clear them out.

She sat on the floor with Jackson. "I need a sample of the blood you're wearing, Jack."

"There's so much of it." His body jerked every few seconds, as if in surprise. "It's not mine."

"No." She took several samples — face, arms, chest, back, feet. "What were you doing in 606?"

"What?"

"Suite 606. You were in there."

"I don't know. Was I?"

"Who's the woman?"

"There were a lot of women, weren't there?" Again he shuddered in pain. "Were you there? Do you know what happened?"

"Look at me, goddamn it." Her voice was like a slap, shocked him back to her. "There's a woman in 606. Her throat's slashed."

"Did I do it? Did I hurt somebody?" He pressed his forehead to his knees. "My head. My head. Somebody's screaming in my head."

"Do you belong to the Asant Group?"

"I don't know. What is it? I don't know. Who are you? What's happening?"

With a shake of her head, Eve rose as the med-techs she'd ordered stepped in. "I want him examined. I want a blood sample. I need to know what he's on. When you're done, he'll be transported to Cop Central."

"Whose blood is it?"

"You're too late for her." She walked back into the living area to leave them to it just as her partner came in the main door.

Peabody's hair was pulled back in a stubby little tail that left her square face unframed and seemed to enlarge her brown eyes. She wore baggy dark pants and a white tee with a red jacket tossed over it. She carried a field kit.

"Who died?"

"An as yet unidentified female. Prime suspect is in there." Eve jerked her head. "Naked and covered with what is most likely her blood."

"Wow. Must've been a hell of a party."

"It happened on the other side. Let's go work the scene."

Outside the doors of 606 they coated hands and feet with Seal-It while Eve gave Peabody the rundown.

"He just walked into the cocktail party? And doesn't remember anything?"

"Yes, and so it seems. He doesn't come off as faking it. Both pupils are big as the moon. He's disoriented, motor skills are off, and he appears to have one major headache."

"Stoned?"

"Be my first guess, but we'll see what the MTs have to say about it." Eve unsealed the door, and now used the key Roarke had acquired for her.

When she stepped in, the sturdy Peabody blanched. "Man. Oh crap." She bent over at the waist, pressed her hands to her thighs and took long, slow breaths.

"Don't you boot on my crime scene."

"Just need a minute. Okay." She kept breathing. "Okay. Black magic. Bad juju."

"Don't start that shit. We've got a bunch of assholes who had an orgy, topped it off with ritual murder using Satan as an excuse. Used the private elevator," Eve added, gesturing toward it, "most likely, coming and going. We'll want the security discs for that. Cleaned up after they did her. Evidence of that in the bathrooms, of which there are six in this place. Beds show signs of being used, and food and drink were consumed. Since I doubt the pentagram is part of the room's original decor, somebody drew it on the floor. A question might be 'Why?' Why use a fancy, high-dollar hotel suite for your annual satanic meeting?

"Let's get her prints, get an ID and a time of death." Since Peabody still looked pale, Eve opted to take the body herself. "Do a run on Pike, Jackson. His prints came up with age thirty-three, and an addy on West Eighty-eighth. He's a doctor. See if he's got a sheet."

Eve stepped over to the body, doing what she could to avoid the blood. Not to preserve her shoes, but the scene. The air chilled, teased gooseflesh on her arms, and once more she felt, sensed, a pulsing.

She lifted the victim's hand to the Identi-pad, scanned the prints.

"Marsterson, Ava, age twenty-six, single. Mixed-race female with an address on Amsterdam. Employed as office manager at the West Side Health Clinic."

Eve tipped her head at the tattoo — a red and gold serpent swallowing its own tail — that circled the left hip. "She's got a tat on her hip, and it's not listed on her ID. Maybe a temp, or maybe fresh."

She took out her gauge. "TOD, twenty-two-ten. That's nearly an hour before Pike crashed the party down the hall." She replaced the gauge and studied the body. "The victim's throat is deeply slashed, in what appears to be a single blow with a sharp blade, right to left, slightly downward angle. A right-handed attacker, facing. He wanted to see your face when he sliced you open. Multiple wounds, slices, stab wounds, over shoulders, torso, abdomen, legs. Varying sizes and depths. Various blades held in various hands? Victim is posed, arms and legs spread, in the center of a black pentagram drawn directly onto the floor. Bruising on the thighs. Possible rape or consensual sex, ME to determine. No defensive wounds. None. Didn't put up a fight, Ava? Did they just take you down by slashing your throat, then have a party on you? Tox screen to determine presence of alcohol and/or drugs."

At the knock on the door, Eve called out for Peabody.

"I got it." Peabody hustled over, used the security peep. "It's Crime Scene."

In minutes the room filled with noise, movement, equipment, and the somehow cleaner smell of chemicals. When the crew from the morgue rolled in, Eve stepped away from the body.

"Marsterson, Ava. Bag and tag. Peabody, with me. Run this Asant Group," she ordered. "We're going in to shake what we can out of Pike."

"There had to be at least a dozen people in there, Dallas. Twelve, fifteen people by the number of trays and the glasses. Why come here to do this? You can't cover it up this way, and hey, party down the hall going on at the same time with a cop right there. By the way, you look totally mag. The shoes are up to wicked."

Eve frowned down at the shoes she'd forgotten she was wearing. "Shit, shit. I've got to go into Central in this get-up." She'd also, she realized, forgotten Roarke.

He leaned against the wall outside Maxia's suite doing something that entertained or interested him on his PPC. And looked up as she approached.

"Sorry. I should've told you to go home."

"I assumed you'd want the code for the car since it's not one of yours. I had the garage bring it out front. Hello, Peabody."

"Hey. You guys look superior. It's really too bad the evening got screwed for you."

"It got screwed bigger for Ava Marsterson," Eve commented. "Maxia?"

"Took a soother and went to bed. I'll get myself home." He caught Eve's chin in his hand, skimmed his thumb down the dent, then kissed her. He handed her a mini memo cube. "Code's on it. Take care, Lieutenant. Good night, Peabody."

Peabody watched him walk away. "Boy, sometimes you just want to slurp him up without a straw." She wheeled her eyes to Eve. "Did I say that out loud?"

CHAPTER
THREE

Grateful she kept some workout gear in her locker, Eve stripped off the party dress, pried her aching feet out of the hated shoes, then pulled on loose cotton pants and a faded gray tee. Since she couldn't walk around Central or successfully intimidate a suspect dripping in diamonds, she had no choice but to secure them in her locker.

Safe enough, she thought. If they'd been a candy bar, odds were lower that her property would be there when she opened the locker. But a small — probably not so small — fortune in diamonds, no problem.

After stepping into an ancient pair of skids, she met Peabody in the corridor.

"No criminal. Nothing, Dallas. He had a detained and released for disturbing the peace when he was twenty. Some college fraternity party. It wouldn't be on his record except the campus cops slapped the whole fraternity over it. He's from Pennsylvania, just moved here a couple of weeks ago. He's a doctor, pretty much brand-spanking-new, and just took a position on staff at —"

"The West Side Health Clinic."

"It's annoying to do the run if I don't get the payoff. Interview A. They got him cleaned up."

"The victim?" Eve asked as they walked.

"Clean to the squeaky level. Moved to New York about two years ago from Indiana. Both parents and younger brother still back there. We'll have to notify them."

"We'll take Pike first. They can wait a few hours to have their lives shattered." She pushed open the door to the interview room, nodded to the uniform.

The uniform stepped out, and Eve walked to the table where Jack sat in the orange pants and shirt of a con. "Record on. Dallas, Lieutenant Eve, and Peabody, Detective Delia, in interview with Pike, Jackson, regarding the investigation into the death of Marsterson, Ava."

"Ava?" Jack looked up, his face squeezed tight as if he struggled on the name. "Ava?"

"That's right, Ava. You've been read your rights, Mr Pike, is that correct?"

"Ah, I don't know."

"Then we'll refresh you." Eve recited the Revised Miranda. "Do you understand your rights and obligations?"

"I think. Yes. Why? Why am I here?"

"You don't remember?"

"My head." He pressed both hands to his temples. "Was I in an accident? My head hurts."

"What do you remember about today?"

"I . . . I went to work. Didn't I? What day is it? Is it Tuesday?"

"It's Wednesday."

"But . . ." Jack stared up at her. "What happened to Tuesday?"

"What drugs did you take, Jack?"

"I don't, I don't take drugs. I don't do illegals. I'm a doctor. I'm on staff at . . ." He held his head again, and rocked. "Where? Where?"

"The West Side Health Clinic."

He looked at Eve, his eyes, his face slack with relief. "Yes. Yes. That's it. I just started. I went to work. I went to work, and then . . ." He moaned, shuddered. "Please, can I have a blocker? My head's pounding."

"You've got something in you, Jack. I can't give you a blocker until I know what it is. Did you go to the Palace Hotel with Ava? To Suite 606?"

"Ava . . . I can't . . . Ava works at the clinic." Sweat shone on his face from the effort. "Ava, manages . . . Ava. We . . ." Then horror covered it. "No. No. No."

"What happened to Ava, Jack?"

"No. No."

"What happened in 606?"

"I don't know. I don't —"

"Stop!" She reached over, grabbed a fistful of his shirt. "You tell me what happened."

"It's not real. It didn't happen."

"What isn't real?"

"The people, the people." He surged to his feet, and Eve signaled Peabody to stay back. "The lights. The voices. Smoke and fire. And hell came." He lurched around the interview room, holding his head. Tears leaked out of his eyes. "Laughing. Screaming. I

27

couldn't stop. Did I want to stop? We had sex. No. Yes. I don't know. Bodies and hands and mouths. They hurt her. Did I hurt her? But she was smiling, smiling at me. Then her blood."

His hands ran over his face as if wiping at it. "Her blood. All over me."

His eyes rolled up in his head. Peabody managed to break the worst of his fall by going down with him. "Jesus, Dallas, no way this guy's faking it."

"No. Let's get him into a cage. I want him on suicide watch. I want eyes on him." She stepped to the door at the knock.

"Screening on your suspect, Lieutenant. They said you wanted it ASAP."

"Thanks." She took the report from a tech, scanned it. "Jesus, what doesn't this guy have in him? Erotica, Rabbit, Zoner, Jive, Lucy."

"Sleepy, Dopey, and Doc," Peabody finished. Then shrugged at Eve's frown. "Bad joke. No wonder his head's screaming. Coming down off a cocktail like that's gotta rip it up."

"Get him into a cage, have a medic treat him. He's had enough for one night."

"He doesn't come across like somebody who could do what was done to that woman tonight."

"That much junk inside him, you don't know what he could do. But he's not a regular user. No way he could be a regular with that kind of habit and not have a single pop."

Eve started back to her office. A couple of uniforms led a weeping woman away in the opposite direction.

Outside the bullpen a guy wearing a torn and bloody shirt sat laughing quietly to himself while he rattled the restraints that chained him to the seat.

She swung into the bullpen while he went back to giggling. In her office she hit the AutoChef for coffee first, then sat at her desk. She gulped caffeine while she booted up the security discs from the hotel.

She ran the VIP check-in first, the elaborate parlor reserved for guests in the tonier suites and the triplexes. She ordered the computer to coordinate with the time stamped on the Asant Group's check-in. And watched the parlor fuzz into white static. She ran it back, noted the glitch began thirty minutes before the log-in, and continued to twenty-three hundred.

The pattern repeated when she ran the security discs for the private elevator, and again when she ran the main lobby discs.

"Son of a bitch." She turned to her interoffice 'link. "Peabody, wake up your cohab. I need McNab in here to dig into the security discs. They're wiped."

If the boy genius from the Electronic Detectives Division couldn't dig out data, she had someone who could. She contacted Roarke.

"Why are you awake?" she demanded when her 'link screen showed him at his desk.

"Why are you?"

"Oh, just a little something about a ritual murder. I thought you'd want to know that all the security discs from your hotel are compromised. Nothing but static on all starting thirty minutes before the log-in for the Asant Group."

"Are you bringing them to me or am I coming to you?"

"I've got McNab coming in, but —"

"I'm on my way."

"Wait. Listen, grab me some work clothes, will you? And my weapon harness, and —"

"I know what you need."

Her screen went black. Pissed off, she thought, and couldn't blame him. She imagined a few heads would roll at Roarke's Palace, and in short order. But meanwhile, she had useless discs on her hands, a suspect with drug-induced memory blanks, and a mutilated body at the morgue.

And it was still shy of dawn.

She opened her murder book, set up her board. According to the hotel records, the Asant Group had booked the triplex two months prior, and secured it with a credit card under the name of Josef Bellor, who carried an address in Budapest.

She fed the data into her computer, ordered a standard run. Only to learn Josef Bellor of Budapest had died there five years before at the ripe age of one hundred and twenty-one.

"Gonna be hard-pressed to get him to pay the bill," she muttered.

One night's booking, she thought, going over the notes. All room service delivered through the suite's AutoChefs or pre-ordered and delivered prior to check-in. Five cases of wine, several pounds of various European cheeses, fancy breads, caviar, pâtés, cream cakes.

No point in ritual murder on an empty stomach.

So they ate, drank, orgied, she thought, pushing up to pace the small space of her office. Popped whatever illegals suited their fancy. Three floors of revelry, sound-proofed high-collar digs with the privacy shades activated.

Would've saved the best for last, she decided. The sacrifice would've been the evening's crescendo.

Just how did a nice girl from Indiana end up the star of the show? How did a transplanted young doctor from Pennsylvania get invited and left behind?

"Lieutenant."

She turned to the sleepy-eyed McNab in her doorway. He wore pants of screaming yellow that matched the fist-sized dots shrieking over a shirt of eye-tearing green. His long blond hair was pulled back from his thin, pretty face into a tail. She wondered if the hank of it somehow balanced the weight of the tangle of silver loops in his ear.

"Doesn't it ever give you a headache?" she wondered. "Just looking in the mirror."

"Huh?"

"Never mind. Discs." She gathered them from her desk, pushed them at him. "Find something on them. Roarke's on his way."

"Okay. Why?"

"They're his discs. Palace Hotel security. I've already shot a report to your unit in EDD. Read it, work it. Get me something."

He stifled a yawn, then focused on her board. "Is that the vic?"

Eve only nodded, said nothing when he came in to study the board. He'd work better and harder, she knew, if he was invested. "That's fucked up," he said. "That's seriously fucked up. And that's gotta be more than one killer." He slipped the discs into one of the pockets of his pants. "If there's an image on these, we'll get it."

If there were no images, she thought when McNab left, it meant the security had been compromised on site. Knowing how tightly any ship in Roarke's expansive fleet ran, that would've taken some serious magic.

She turned toward her 'link with the idea of tagging Roarke on his way in. And he walked into her office.

"That was quick."

"I'm in a hurry." He set a bag on her visitor's chair. "Where are the discs?"

"I just passed them off to McNab. Wait." She shot out a hand as he turned. "If the security was breached on site, how could it be done?"

"I don't know until I see the discs, do I?"

"Be pissed off later. How could it be done?"

He made an obvious effort to settle himself, then walked to her AutoChef to program coffee for himself. "It would have to be through security or electronics, and one of the top levels. Most likely both, working in tandem. No one at that level would consider a bribe of any kind worth their position."

"Threat, blackmail?"

"Anything's possible, of course, but doubtful. It would be more to their advantage to come to me with the problem than to circumvent security."

"I'll need names anyway."

He set the coffee aside, took out his PPC. After a moment's work, he nodded toward her machine. "Now you have them. And if any of my people had a part in what happened to that girl, I want to know when you know."

He walked out, his barely restrained fury leaving a bolt of energy behind. Eve blew out a breath, and since he'd forgotten his coffee, picked it up and drank it herself.

CHAPTER
FOUR

Though she had no doubt Roarke's screening process was more stringent than the Pentagon's, she ran the names he'd given her. She got clean and clear on all. If, she decided, the word from EDD was an on site screwup, she'd run their spouses, when applicable, and family members.

But for now she couldn't put off informing next of kin.

It took, Eve thought when she'd finished, under thirty seconds to shatter the world of two ordinary people, with ordinary lives. More time, she reflected as she turned back to her board, than it had taken to slash Ava Marsterson's throat, for her brain to process the insult. But not much. Not much more.

She rubbed the heels of her hands over eyes gritty with fatigue, then checked the time. A couple of hours until she could bitch at the lab for any results, or go to the morgue for the same on the victim's autopsy.

Enough time for a shower to clear her head before nagging EDD. She picked up the bag Roarke had left her.

"Take two hours in the crib," she ordered Peabody when she stepped back into the bullpen. "I'm going to grab a shower."

"Okay. I ran the Asant Group from every possible angle. It doesn't exist."

"It's just a cover."

"Then I tried a search for any occult holidays, or dates of import that coordinate with today — or yesterday now. Nothing."

"Well, that was good thinking. Worth a shot. It was a damn party, that's for sure. Maybe they don't need an occasion. No, no," Eve corrected herself. "It was too elaborate, planned too far in advance to just be for the hell of it."

"For the hell of it. Ha-ha. God." Peabody rubbed her eyes. "I need those two hours down."

"Take them now. It's the last you'll be seeing of the back of your eyelids for a while."

She headed to the showers. In the locker room she checked the contents of the bag, noted that Roarke hadn't missed a trick. Underwear, boots, pants, shirt, jacket, weapon harness, her clutch piece, communicator, restraints, spare recorder, PPC, and cash. More than she normally carried on the job. She stuffed it all in her locker, grabbed a towel, then wrapped herself in it once she'd stripped off.

In the miserly shower cube she ordered the water on full at 101 degrees. It came out in a stingy lukewarm trickle, so she closed her eyes and pretended she was home, where the shower sported multiple and generous jets that pummeled the body with glorious heat. Then spun around, soaking wet, when her instincts tingled to see Roarke standing in the narrow opening, hands in pockets.

"If this is the best the NYPSD offers it's no wonder you're prone to hour-long showers at home."

"What's wrong with you? Close the door. Anybody could walk in here."

"I locked the door, which you neglected to do."

"Because cops aren't prone to sneaking peeks while another cop is in the damn shower. What are you doing?"

"Taking my clothes off so they don't get wet. That's the usual procedure."

"You can't come in here." She jabbed a finger at him when he draped his shirt over a bench. "Cut it out. There's barely room for me. Besides —"

"The security was breached on site. It's going to be a very long day. I want a shower, and since she's naked, wet, and here, I want my wife."

He stepped in, slid his arms around her. "Not only is this excuse for a shower stall the approximate size of a coffin, but it's bloody noisy for the amount of water dripping out."

"Who's the most likely to have compromised —"

"Later," he said, and drew her in. "Later," and covered her mouth with his.

She'd seen his eyes before their lips met; seen the worry and the fatigue in them. It was so rare for him to show either, even to her, that she instinctively wrapped around him. Need. She understood the need, not just for the physical, but for the unity.

Touch, taste, movement. Knowing who you were, each to the other, and what you became when that need brought you together.

"Anybody finds out about this," she murmured in his ear, "I'll get razzed for years." She bit lightly at his lobe. "So make it good."

Her heart slammed against her ribs when he drove into her. "Okay. That's a start."

He laughed, an unexpected and welcome zing of humor along with the pleasure. The old pipes clanged and rattled as he slowed his thrusts, smoothed the pace down from urgent to easy. He turned his head, found her mouth again, and drew them both down, deep, deep. Filled them both from the shimmering well of sensation and emotion.

He felt her rise up, the cry of her release tangled in the kiss. And let himself follow.

On a long, long breath, she dropped her head on his shoulder. "This is not authorized use of departmental facilities."

"We expert civilian consultants need our perks, too." He tipped her head up. "I adore you, Lieutenant."

"Yeah? Then shove it over some, pal. You're hogging what there is of the water."

When they stepped out and she began toweling off, he lifted a brow. "Towel over drying tube? Not your usual."

"I don't trust them in here." She gave the tube a suspicious glare. "You could get fried, or maybe worse, trapped. Anyway, I gave Peabody some crib time, but

I'm going to cut it short, see if they've gotten to the vic at the morgue."

"I'll be going with you."

She didn't argue; it was a waste of time. "You're not responsible for what happened to Ava Marsterson."

He watched her as he buttoned his shirt. "If you put one of your men in charge of an op, and there was a screwup, if a civilian lost her life, who does it fall on?"

She sat to pull on her boots, tried another way. "No security, not even yours, is completely infallible."

He sat beside her on the bench. "A group of people came into my place, breached the security from the inside, and ripped a woman to pieces. I need to know how, and I need to know why. If one of my people was part of it, I'm going to know who."

"Then I'd better roust Peabody. I hope you came down in my ride," she added. "That toy we drove last night won't hold the three of us."

"I drove something that will."

"This is so mag!" Peabody bounced on the backseat of the muscular and roomy all-terrain. "First we get to zip in that way-uptown Stinger, and now we're pumping the road in this."

"Glad you're enjoying yourself," Eve commented. "We wouldn't want murder to dampen your day."

"You've got to take your ups where you get them. I've never even seen one of these before." Peabody petted the seat as she might a purring cat.

"It's a prototype," Roarke told her. "It won't go on line for a couple of months yet."

"Sweetness."

"Peabody, as soon as you finish enjoying yourself, run the heads of security and electronics in the file. Run their spouses, parents, siblings, cohabs, offspring, spouses and cohabs of offspring. I want to know if anyone has a sheet. I want to know if anyone's family pet has a sheet."

"They've been screened," Roarke told her. "Caro can forward you all the data."

Eve had no doubt his efficient admin could gather and transmit data in record time. "We need to confirm, and confirm through official channels."

When he said nothing, she took out her own PPC, copied all data to Dr Mira's office unit. She wanted the department's top profiler and psychiatrist to review and analyze. Added to it, Eve thought, one of Mira's daughters was Wiccan. Maybe, just maybe, they'd tap that source.

The cold white tiles of the morgue echoed with their footsteps. Eve scented coffee — or what passed for it here — as they strode past Vending. She scented death long before they pushed through the double doors of the autopsy room.

Ava lay naked on a slab with Chief Medical Examiner Morris working on her. His delicate and precise Y-cut opened her, exposed her. Eve heard Peabody swallow hard behind her.

Morris straightened as they came in. The protective gown covered his silver-edged blue suit. He wore his dark hair pulled back in a long, sleek tail. "Company," he said, and the faintest of smiles moved across his exotically sexy face. "And so early in the morning. Roarke, this is unexpected." But his eyes tracked over to Peabody. "There's water in the friggie, Detective."

"Thanks." Her face glowed with sweat as she hurried over for a bottle.

"What can you tell me?" Eve asked him.

"We haven't gotten very far. You flagged her for me specifically, and I've only been in about an hour. And that's because the ME on duty was pissy that he couldn't get his hands in."

"I didn't want anyone but you on her. I'd rather wait. I have a pretty good idea how it went anyway. Can you tell me if she was raped?"

"I can tell you she had rough sex — very rough — multiple times. As to whether it was consensual or not? She can't tell us. But from the tearing, I'd say rape. Gang rape."

"Sperm?"

"They doused her — vaginally, anally, orally to remove. I've already sent samples to the lab, but I wouldn't hold my breath for DNA. I'd say multiple partners. She was brutally used, pre-and postmortem." He looked down at the body. "There are so many levels of cruelty, aren't there? And they all walk in our doors."

"What about the tat? It looked fresh and real."

"It's both. Inked within the last twelve to fifteen hours."

"They wanted her marked," Eve mused. "The throat wound came first. Death blow. Right-handed assailant, facing."

"If I were a teacher, you'd be my pet. There are sixty-eight other wounds, several of which would have been mortal on their own, some of which are relatively superficial. I want to run a closer analysis, but on a first pass, at least a dozen different blades were used on her. The bruising, from finger grips, hands, fists, feet. Some pre-mortem. And yet —"

"Not one defensive wound," Eve finished. "No sign she was restrained. She took it. I need to know what she took or what they gave her."

"I've flagged the tox screen priority. I can tell you she wasn't a user, unless it was very rare, very casual. This was a very healthy woman, one who tended to her body, inside and out. There'll be a rape drug in her, something potent enough to cause her to tolerate this kind of abuse without a struggle."

"I've got somebody in the tank. He was loaded. I sent a sample to the lab. Her parents and her brother are coming in from Indiana."

"God pity them." Morris touched one sealed and bloodied hand to Ava's arm. "I'll see she's cleaned up before they view her." Morris glanced over at Roarke, with understanding in his dark eyes. "We'll take care of her," he said. "And them. You can be sure of it."

As they walked down the white-tiled tunnel, Roarke spoke for the first time. "It's a hard life you've chosen, Lieutenant. A brutal road that brings you to that so often."

"It chose me," she said, but was grateful to step outside, and into the cool air of the new spring morning.

CHAPTER
FIVE

Eve gave Roarke an Upper West Side address when they got back into the AT.

"Mika Nakamura's worked for me for nine years." He pulled out of the parking slot. "Four of those as head of security at the hotel."

"Then she must be good," Eve commented. "And should be able to explain what the hell went wrong last night. She was on the log from noon until just after twenty-three hundred. Do you usually work your people for an eleven-hour stretch?"

"No. She should have logged out at eight." His eyes stayed on the road, his voice remained cool and flat. "Paul Chambers came on at seven. I spoke with him last night, and again this morning. He took the main hotel as Mika told him she'd handle the VIP and Towers, as she had other work to catch up on. She also told him she'd be running some maintenance on the cams."

"Is that usual?"

"As head of security, Mika would have some autonomy. She's earned it."

Touchy, Eve thought. *Very touchy.* "Have you spoken with her?"

"I haven't been able to reach her. And, yes, I fully intended to see her in person before you contacted me about the discs." The tone, very cool, very level, spoke of ruthlessly restrained fury. "She wouldn't hold the position she does if she hadn't passed the initial screening, and the twice yearly screening thereafter."

In the backseat, Peabody cleared her throat. "She comes up clean. So does her husband of five years. One child, female, age three. Um, born in Tokyo, and relocated to New York at age ten when her parents — who also come clean — moved here for career purposes. Attended both Harvard and Columbia. Speaks three languages and holds degrees in Communications, Hotel Management, and Psychology."

"How did she end up yours?" Eve asked Roarke.

"I recruited her right out of college. I have scouts, you could call them, and they brought her to my attention. It's not in the realm of any reality that she had any part in what was done to that girl."

"She logged out about ten minutes before Pike walked into Maxia's party. And minutes before the security for the elevators and lobby cleared. We have to look at that. She could've been forced, threatened."

"There are fail-safes." He shook his head. "She's smart. She's too damn smart to get herself trapped that way."

Better to let it lie, Eve decided, until they spoke to the woman in question.

Security paid well enough, in Roarke's domain, to warrant a tidy duplex in a tony neighborhood. People clipped along the sidewalk wearing suits and style while they sipped what she assumed was fancy fake coffee out of go-cups. Pretty women with bouncy hair herded pretty children toward what, she assumed again, would be private schools. A couple of teenagers whizzed by on air-boards while a third chased after them on street blades.

Eve climbed the short steps to the door. "You can take the lead with her," she told Roarke, "but when I step in, you have to step back."

Rather than respond, he rang the bell.

Privacy screens shielded the front windows, and the security lock held a steady red. As the seconds ticked away, Eve wondered how a woman might go into the wind with a husband and a kid. They had a weekend home in Connecticut, she mused, and relatives in Japan. If . . .

The security light blinked green.

Mika Nakamura was a stunner. Eve had seen that from the ID shot. But at the moment, she looked hard used. Sallow skin, dull bloodshot eyes, the tangled mess of ebony hair all spoke of a hard night, or an illness.

"Sir?" the voice rasped. Mika cleared her throat, opened the door a bit wider. She wore a long scarlet robe messily tied at the waist.

"I need to speak with you, Mika."

"Of course. Yes. Is something wrong?"

She stepped back. Eve noted the house was dim, that the privacy screens had been boosted up to block the light. Even so, the interior was splashed with vibrant colors from rugs and art.

"Please come in. Won't you sit down? Can I get you some coffee? Tea?"

"Aren't you well, Mika?"

"I'm just a little off. I had my husband take Aiko out for breakfast because I can't seem to pull it together."

"Long night?" Eve asked, and Mika gave her a puzzled look.

"I . . . sorry?"

"My wife, Lieutenant Dallas, and her partner, Detective Peabody. I've been trying to reach you, Mika."

"You have?" She pushed her hands at her hair in an absent attempt to straighten it. "Nothing's come through. Did I . . ." She pressed her fingers to her temple. "Did I turn the 'links off? Why would I do that?"

"Sit down." Roarke took her arm, led her to a chair in as bold a red as her robe. He sat on the glossy black coffee table to face her. "There was an incident at the hotel last night."

"An incident." She repeated the words slowly, as if learning the language.

"You were on the com, Mika. You ordered Paul to cover the main hotel, though it was already covered. And you dismissed the tech from the screen room, telling them you'd be running some maintenance on the cameras."

"That doesn't sound right." She rubbed at her temple again. "It doesn't sound right."

Eve touched Roarke's shoulder, and though impatience flashed into his eyes, he rose. Eve took his place. "Just before sixteen hundred, you shut down the cameras in the VIP lobby and the private elevator for Suite 606. They remained off until approximately twenty-three hundred."

"Why would I do that?"

Not a denial, Eve noted. A sincere question. "A group checked into that suite. The Asant Group. Do you know them?"

"No."

"During the time the cameras were shut down, from your com, a woman was murdered in that suite."

Even the sickly color faded from Mika's cheeks. "Murdered? Oh, God. Sir —"

"Look at me, Mika," Eve demanded. "Who told you to turn off the cameras, to send your relief away, to dismiss the tech?"

"Nobody." Her breath went short as her pale face bunched with pain. "I didn't. I wouldn't. Murdered? Who? How?"

Eve narrowed her eyes. "Got a headache, Mika?"

"Yes. It's splitting. I took a blocker, but it hasn't touched it. I can't think. I don't understand any of this."

"Do you remember going to work yesterday?"

"Of course. Of course I do. I . . ." Her lips trembled; her eyes filled. "No. No. I don't remember. I don't remember anything, it's all blurred and blank. My head. God." She dropped it into her hands, rocked herself, much as Jackson Pike had. "When I try to remember, it's worse. I can't stand the pain. Sir, something's wrong with me. Something's wrong."

"All right now, Mika." Roarke simply nudged Eve aside, crouched, and put his arms around the weeping woman. "We'll take care of it. We'll get you to a doctor."

"Peabody, help Ms Nakamura get dressed. We'll have her taken down to Central."

"Damn it, Eve." Roarke shoved to his feet.

"Dr Mira can examine her," Eve said evenly, "and determine if the cause is physical or psychological. Or both."

Roarke eased back, turned to help Mika to her feet. "Go with Detective Peabody. It's going to be all right."

"Someone's dead. Did I do something? If I did —"

"Look at me. It's going to be all right."

It seemed to calm her. But as she continued to tremble, Peabody put an arm around her to lead her from the room.

"Same symptoms as Jackson Pike," Eve commented. "Down the line."

"Eve —"

"I'm cutting you a break by not getting pissed off. Don't push it."

He merely nodded. "I'll stay until she's ready to go. Then I've other things to see to."

"Good." She took out her communicator to arrange for Mika's transportation, then contacted Mira's office. She plowed through Mira's admin. "I'm pulling rank, are you hearing me? If necessary I'll go to the commander on this, and nobody'll be happy about that. I'm ordering a priority. Dr Mira will clear her schedule as of now. Jackson Pike, currently in custody, will be brought down to her for examination. She has the file. If she has any questions, she can reach me. In an hour, she will examine Mika Nakamura, who will be brought to Central shortly. If you have a problem, you can take it up with me later, but you'll do exactly what I've told you, and you'll do it now."

Eve clicked off. "Ought to hook her up with Summerset." she muttered. "Couple of tight-asses." While Roarke watched thoughtfully, she contacted her own division and arranged for two uniforms to deliver Pike to Mira's office, ASAP. Satisfied, she shoved the communicator back in her pocket.

"Someone used her," Roarke began.

"Maybe."

"Used her," he repeated. "And a woman's dead because of it. Mika won't ever forget that."

"You can worry about that now. I can't."

"Understood. We're not on different sides, Eve. Just slightly different angles. She's in pain, and afraid, and confused. And she's mine. You understand that."

"Yeah." She understood that right down to the bone. "And Ava Marsterson's mine. Do I think your head of security suddenly thought it would be fun to help a bunch of lunatics carve someone up in the name of Satan? No. But there's a reason they used her, a reason they used your place, that room, that victim. There's a reason for Jackson Pike."

Eve stepped over as Peabody led Mika back into the room.

"Ms Nakamura, do you use the West Side Health Clinic?"

"What? Yes. Aiko's pediatrician is there, and my doctor."

"Do you know Ava Marsterson?"

"I —" Mika staggered back, one hand pressed to her head. "Who? I can't think through the pain."

Eve glanced at Roarke. "I take that as a yes."

"She's straight, Dallas." Peabody brooded out the window of the AT. "She could barely stand for the pain, but she fought to push through it. Worried about her husband and kid, sick — seriously sick — at the idea someone died while she had the com." She glanced at Eve. "Just like Pike. So you have to think, given the circumstances . . . Ritual magic, on the black side, the gathering of, well, power. By all appearances and all evidence, the ability to cause two straight arrows to behave in a way opposed to their character. We could be dealing with a spell."

Eve's brown eyes narrowed. "I knew you were going to get around to that."

"It's not unprecedented," Peabody insisted. "There are sensitives, unscrupulous sensitives who've used their gifts for their own gain, their own purpose. Black magic's taking those gifts, that power, and distorting it."

"Jackson Pike was loaded with drugs."

"Add drugs to the mix, it's easier to bend the will. There was something in that suite, something left over." Peabody rubbed her arms as if suddenly chilled. "You felt it, too."

She didn't argue, because that much was true. "I'm not buying that some witch can . . ." Eve waved a hand in the air. "And get some normal guy to start hacking someone with a knife."

"I don't think he did. I think he was supposed to be another sacrifice — or maybe just the patsy." When Eve didn't respond, Peabody scowled. "You don't want to buy into the power deal, but going straight logic, why does this group plan all this and include some young doctor who's only been in New York a couple of weeks, and has no ties, *none* to anything off prior to that? You don't bring some newbie in on the big deal. You don't —"

"You're right."

"Listen, I'm just saying . . . I'm right?"

"About Pike, yeah, you're right. Maybe they were going to off him, too. Or maybe they pulled him in to take the rap. Drugged the shit out of him, left him behind. He's got no defense. Naked, full of illegals, covered with the vic's blood, and carrying around one of the knives used on her. Still, they'd have to figure we'd know he didn't do it alone, and once the drugs wear off, we examine him, work with him, he could start to remember some details."

Peabody pondered on it a moment. "Okay, look, you don't buy the magic, but you'll agree that people who get together to light candles, have orgies that end in human sacrifice, probably do."

"I'll give you that."

"And can be persuasive — especially if they have a gift, are a sensitive, especially if the person they're persuading is doped up."

"Okay, Eve nodded.

"So, to *dissuade* we need someone with a gift, someone who believes, to break the spell."

"You want to bring in a witch? Christ."

"It's an option," Peabody pushed.

"Mira's going to examine them, and determine the root of the physical and/or psychological blocks. Let's stick with reality, for just a little while."

She shot up to a slot on a second-level street parking. "Trosky, Brian, on the desk at the time of the group check-in. Let's see what he remembers, or if he's got himself a really bad headache this morning."

Eve strode across the sidewalk and into the apartment building. As it didn't boast a doorman or clerk, she went straight to the intercoms, pressed the one labeled TROSKY.

When no response came, Eve bypassed the elevator lock. "Third floor," she ordered.

The music blasted out the moment the doors opened on three. A woman stood beating on the door of 305, Trosky's apartment. "Brian, for chrissake, turn it *down!*"

"Problem?" Eve asked at close to a shout.

"Yeah, unless you're frigging deaf. He's had that music blaring like that for over an hour. I work nights. I gotta get some sleep."

"He doesn't answer the door? Did you try his 'link?"

"Yeah. It's not like him, I gotta say. He's a nice guy. Good neighbor." She beat on the door again. "Brian, for chrissake!"

"Okay, move aside."

51

When Eve pulled out her master, the woman goggled. "Hold on, hold on a minute. You can't just go breaking into somebody's place. I'm calling the cops."

"We are the cops." Eve nodded at Peabody as she used the master, and Peabody pulled out her badge.

"Oh, wow, oh, shit. Is he in trouble? I don't wanna get him in trouble."

Eve pushed open the door, felt her eardrums vibrate at the force of the music. "Mr Trosky, this is the police!" she shouted. "We're coming in. Music, off," she ordered, but the roar of it continued. "Peabody, find the source of that noise and kill it. Trosky! This is the NYPSD!"

She drew her weapon, but kept it down at her side as she scanned the living area — trashed — then the bump-out of the kitchen. She moved to the open bedroom door.

He lay across the bed, tangled in the bloody sheets. She swept the room and the adjoining bath, though instinct told her Brian Trosky hadn't been attacked, that the hammer that had caved his skull — to stop the pain? — had been wielded by his own hand.

CHAPTER
SIX

Same side, Roarke thought as he walked into Spirit Quest, *different angles*. Eve would always search for the logical, the rational. He was a bit more flexible. And so he'd come to talk to the witch.

The shop was pretty, even festive in its way with its crystals and stones, its bells and candles, its colorful bowls and thriving herbs. Its scent was spring meadow, he thought, with a hint of moonlight.

In the small space with the murmur of harps and flutes as background, people browsed. He watched a woman in a flowing white dress carry a ball of smoky crystal to the counter where the young, fresh-faced clerk instructed her solemnly on how to charge the ball by moonlight, how to cleanse it.

When the purchase had been made, wrapped and bagged, Roarke took a step toward the counter. He needn't have bothered, as she stepped out of the back room with an awareness in her dark eyes that told him she'd sensed him — or in the more pedestrian method, had seen him on a security screen.

"Welcome back."

"Isis." He took the hand she offered, held it — and yes, felt that frisson of something. Some connection.

"You're not here to shop," she said in her warm, throaty voice, "which is too bad considering the depths of your pockets. Come upstairs, we'll be comfortable and you can tell me what you need to know."

She led the way, through the back, up the stairs. She moved gracefully, athletically, an Amazon goddess of considerable height and generous curves. Her flaming hair fell in mad curls nearly to the waist of the snug white top she wore, just teasing the back of the first of the many layers of her skirt, a rainbow of hues. She turned at the door, smiled at him out of those onyx eyes. Her face was bold, broad featured with skin of a dull, dreamy gold.

"Once, in another life, we sought comfort together for more than talk." Her smile faded. "But now it's death, again it's death that brings you here. And weighs on you. I'm sorry."

She stepped into the living area of an apartment as exotic and appealing as her shop. "Your Eve is well?"

"Yes. Chas?"

She let out a laugh. "Snuck down to the deli for coffee," she said, referring to her lover. "We pretend he's having a walk. But you can't live with and love another and not know at least some of their secrets."

He stared into her dark eyes, so compelling — so eerily familiar. "Did I know yours, once upon a time?"

She gestured to a chair, took her own. "We knew each other, and loved very well. But I was not your love, your only. You found her then, as you've found her again. And always will. You knew when you first saw her. At the first scent, the first touch."

"I did. It was . . ." He smiled a little, remembering his first contact with Eve. "Annoying."

"Does she know you've come?"

"No. We don't always follow the same lines, even though we usually end in the same place. I don't know if you can help, or if I have a right to bring death to your door."

"Not ordinary death." Isis took a long, slow breath. "Has someone used the arts to cause harm?"

"I don't know. They have, at least, used the illusion of them to kill an innocent woman. You haven't heard of this?"

"We've only just opened this morning, and I don't listen to the media reports." Rings glittered and gleamed on her fingers as she laid her hands on the arms of her chair, settled back. "What would I have heard?"

He told her then, watched her lovely skin pale, her eyes go darker yet. "Do you know of them? The Asant Group?"

"No, and I would have." Her fingers stroked the smooth blue stone of the pendant she wore, as if for comfort. "I hear both the dark and the light. Suite 606. Or 666 with such little change. You didn't know this girl?"

"No."

"You brought nothing of hers, nothing she owned, wore, touched?"

"I'm sorry, no."

Still pale, Isis nodded. "Then to help you, you need to take me there. To where they sacrificed her."

★　★　★

Eve shot over to the West Side Clinic. "They had to troll for the victim here. Scoop up the new doctor, connect with Mika. Somebody on staff, a patient, one of the goddamn cleaning crew."

"Do you really think Pike or Mika might try to kill themselves like Trosky?"

"Mira's notified. It won't happen. It's not even noon," Eve replied.

"Sure could use lunch though."

"Maybe he did slip out on them, or came to sooner than they figured. Walked into the party. Impromptu party, Maxia just planned it the day before. Couldn't know he'd walk right into another penthouse. Couldn't know a cop and the owner of the hotel would be right there, that we'd find the body minutes later."

"Without the party he might've wandered around the floor for hours, or . . . gotten down to a lower floor, even the lobby," Peabody agreed. "Nobody would've zeroed right in on 606."

"What you'd get is a lot of civilian screaming, running, security taking him down. Cops get called in. At some point, they're going to check the discs, but they don't know the exact time frame, so it'd take a while, and a while longer to pinpoint 606 and find her. If three of the key players kill themselves before we interview them thoroughly, before they're examined by a professional, what've we got?"

"What looks like the new guy in town luring a pretty girl to her death, and being in league with the other two, being part of a cult."

"Yeah, you could waste some time on that. They may not be ready for us." Eve swung toward the curb, coldly double-parking. "Not quite ready." She flipped on her On Duty sign, stepped out, and walked to the clinic.

Babies cried. Why, she wondered, did they always sound like invading aliens? People sat with the dead-eyed stare of the ill or the terminally bored. Eve crossed over to the check-in desk where a brunette looked at her with tear-ravaged eyes.

"I'm sorry, we're not taking walk-ins today. I can refer you to —" She broke off when Eve laid her badge on the counter. "Oh. Oh. Ava." Tears popped out, fat and fast. "It's about Ava."

"Who's in charge here?"

"I — I — Ava really managed the clinic. She really handled everything. I don't understand how —"

"Sarah." Another woman in a smart suit stepped up, touched the receptionist's shoulder. "Go on into the break-room for a little while. It's all right."

"I'm sorry, Leah. I just can't *stand* it." She rose, fled.

"I'm Leah Burke." The older brunette held out a hand, gave Eve's a firm shake. "One of the nurse practitioners. We only heard about Ava a couple of hours ago. We're all just . . . Well, we're reeling. Please, come back. I need to find someone to cover the desk. We can use Dr Slone's office, he's with a patient. Left, then right, then the third door on the right. I'll be right with you."

Eve tried to ignore the images of what might be going on behind the closed doors of examination rooms. She hated clinics, hospitals, doctors, MTs. If they were medicals, she wanted them to keep their damn distance.

Slone's office was polished and prim. Diplomas in black frames made the walls important, while a photo of a hot blonde on the desk added that personal touch. Sturdy, straight-back chairs ranged in back and in front of the wide desk.

"Run her," Eve told Peabody.

"Already am. Forty-eight years old, divorced. One child, female, deceased. Aw, jeez, hit while crossing the street. Drunk driver. Graduated Columbia Medical School. Put in ten years at the free clinic in Alphabet City, took five years as professional mother, did another two in Alphabet City, unemployed for a year after her kid died, then came here. Six years in. No criminal. She —"

At Eve's signal, Peabody lowered her PPC. A moment later Leah hurried in. "I'm very sorry. We're all turned around and upset today. We're scrambling to reschedule appointments, and deal with patients when we can't. Do you want Ava's medical and employment records? Dr Collins authorized us to turn them over to the police if you came for them."

"Yeah, we'll take them. And Dr Pike's."

"Jack?" She seemed to sink. "We were afraid . . . We haven't been able to reach him, and he didn't come in for his shift. They were together last night. Their first date."

"Is that so?"

"Ava was so nervous, and Jack was so sweet. I can't believe they're dead."

"She is; he isn't. Where were they going?"

"What? He's all right?" Her eyes widened, went shiny with tears. "Jack's all right?"

"He'll do. Do you know where they were going?"

"Ah, just something casual. Dinner and vid, maybe a club. What happened? Can you tell us what happened? The reports don't make any sense, and when we call for information, we can't get any. We're all —"

She stepped aside as the door opened. He was an imposing man, maybe six-two, lean as a whip with a sharply chiseled face. His eyes were green with a touch of gold, his hair a deep bronze.

"Dr Slone, this is ... I'm sorry, I'm so turned around. I didn't get the names. The police."

"Lieutenant Dallas, Detective Peabody."

"Yes, of course. Leah, see to Sarah, will you? She should go home." He went to his desk, sat behind it. "What happened to Ava?"

"She was murdered."

"Mutilated, the reports say. The word was 'mutilated'."

"That would be accurate."

He breathed slowly in, slowly out. "In a hotel room. I find it hard to believe Ava would go to a hotel room with Jack on a first date. With anyone for that matter."

"She was a young healthy woman. Young healthy women often go to hotel rooms on a date."

"She was shy, and what I'm sure you'd think of as old-fashioned." The flare of anger brought out the gold in his eyes. "She must have been forced to go there, and Jack would never force her, or anyone. Where is Dr Pike?"

"He's in custody."

Now Slone rose from his seat. "You've arrested him? For this?"

"I said he was in custody, not that he was under arrest."

Disdain tightened his face as he stared holes through Eve. "Does he have a lawyer?"

"He hasn't requested one."

"I won't have that boy accused of this. I brought him here. Do you understand? I brought him here."

"You recruited him," Eve said, thinking of Roarke's earlier statement.

"He's a fine doctor, a fine young man. A healer, not a killer. I'll personally arrange for his counsel."

"That's your choice. Where were you last night, Dr Slone?"

"I beg your pardon?"

Eve often wondered why people used that phrase when they really meant "fuck you".

"It's routine. What time did you leave the clinic?"

"I left about four, and walked home. I believe I arrived close to five."

"Can anyone verify that? Your wife, your staff?"

"It was our housekeeper's day off," he said stiffly. "My wife was out. She got home shortly after seven. I resent the implications of this."

"I'm going to implicate the same to the rest of the staff and employees of the clinic. I can use your office, or conduct the implications downtown."

"We'll see what my lawyer has to say about that."

Before he could reach for his 'link, Eve snatched Peabody's bag, and pulled out the still of Ava at the crime scene.

"Take a look, take a good one." Eve slapped the photo on his desk. "Then curl your lip at my *implications* and call your damn lawyer."

He didn't pale; he didn't tremble. But he looked for a very long time. And when he raised his head his eyes were hard, and they were cold. "She was hardly more than a child. Use the office. I'll notify the others. They'll have to speak with you between patients."

He strode out, shut the door behind him.

"He's got a mean bedside manner," Eve commented.

"So do you, sir."

With a shrug, Eve dipped her hands into her pockets. "Run him. Run them all."

CHAPTER
SEVEN

While Isis gathered what she needed, Roarke took out his 'link to contact Eve. He struggled against the resentment that burned through him at the idea he felt obligated to get clearance from his wife to enter his own property. And, he realized, resented the struggle *against* the resentment.

Bloody cops, he thought, *and their bloody procedure.* And then, *bloody hell* when he was dumped straight to her voicemail.

"Well then, if you can't be bothered to answer your 'link, I'll tell you that I've my own expert. I want her to have a pass at the crime scene, so I'll be taking her there shortly. Any problem with that, well, you'll have to get back to me, won't you? And we'll see if I can be bothered answering my 'link."

When he clicked off he saw Isis watching him with amusement dancing in her eyes. "Two strong-headed, strong-willed people, both not only used to giving orders but to having them obeyed. It must be an interesting and stimulating life you have together."

"There are times I wonder how we ever managed to get through two hours together much less two years.

And other times I wonder how either of us survived before we found each other."

"She'll be angry with you for taking me to this place."

"No, what she'll be is right pissed. But they used my place, you see, and at least one of my people. So pissed she'll have to be. I'm grateful to you for doing this."

"Gifts aren't free. What I have, what I am, makes its own demands. Will you take this?" She held out a small white silk bag tied with silver cord.

"What is it?"

"A protection charm. I'd like you to carry it when we go in that room together."

"All right." He slipped it in his pocket, felt it bump lightly against the gray button he habitually carried there. Eve's button, he mused, and wasn't that a kind of charm? "I've been in before."

"Yes. And what did you feel?"

"Beyond the anger, the pity? I suppose if I were a fanciful man I'd say I caught the scent of hell. It's not sulphur and brimstone. It's the stench of cruelty."

Isis took a long breath. "Then we'll go. And we'll look."

In Slone's office, Eve glanced at the readout on her 'link, and let the transmission go to voicemail. Roarke would have to wait, she decided, and turned back to Sarah Meeks. The receptionist had a soother in her now, but tears still trembled.

"Where were Ava and Jack going?"

"They weren't sure. They both wanted to keep it light, you know? First date, and you work in the same place, so if it doesn't work out . . ."

"Did they leave together, from here?"

"No — I mean, I don't think so. She was — they were — still here when I left. But I know she planned to go home first. Even though it was casual, Ava wanted to fuss a little, so she was going home to change."

"What time did you leave?"

"About three. I came on at seven yesterday, and left around three."

"Who else was here when you left?"

"Oh, let's see. Dr Slone, and Dr Collins, and Dr Pratt. Um, Leah, Kiki, Rodney, one of our physician assistants, and . . ."

Eve took notes as Sarah listed names.

"Was Ava seeing anyone else?"

"No. I mean, she dated sometimes, but not a lot, and nothing serious. There was just this spark, you know, between her and Jack. We all thought they might . . ."

"Did she have any interest in the occult?"

"The what? You mean, like ghosts or something?"

"Or something."

"I don't think so. Ava was . . ." She trailed off again, as if trying to find the word. "Grounded. That's it. She was just really real. She loved her job here, and was so good at it. Good with the staff, the patients. She remembered people's names, and what they came in for, and what everybody liked in their coffee."

"Was there anyone who showed a particular interest in her — other than Jack?"

"Everyone did. She was like that. Everybody loved Ava."

Eve sent Sarah out, sniffling. "Anything pop on those runs?" she asked Peabody.

"Nothing that sings. You've got a lot of highly educated people on staff. Slone's married, two kids, no criminal. Wife's an interior designer. Homes in the city, in the Hamptons, and in Colorado. Collins, Dr Lawrence, second marriage, two offspring from each, no criminal. Current wife is professional mother. Upper West Side digs here, and a home in Costa Rica. Pratt —"

"Copy the data to my pocket unit." Eve paced the office. "This is going to take a while. We need to split up. Go over and check Ava's apartment. Have EDD pick up her electronics. I'll meet you back at Central when we're done here."

"Okay. You know, Dallas, we're both going to need sleep at some point."

"We'll get to that. Tell them to get someone else in here."

At least one of the killers was here, Eve thought. She was sure of it. The vic hadn't been in the city two full years, and from what Eve had learned, most of her time and energy and interest funnelled into her work. These were her contacts, her people.

Pike, brand-spanking-new.

It was possible they'd run afoul of someone at Ava's apartment — and Peabody would ferret that out, if so. But logic said both Ava and Jack had known at least one of her killers well enough to trust.

And what easier place was there to drug someone than in a health center? The place was full of drugs — and people who, in Eve's opinion, just loved sticking them into other people. Subdue them here, she speculated, give them enough happy juice to make them compliant and transport them to the hotel, where one or more partners has already dealt with Mika and Trosky.

Get them upstairs, she imagined, and let the party begin. Had to be early. The whole thing had been done by twenty-three hundred, latest. It took time to eat, drink, orgy, and perform a human sacrifice.

She glanced up as the door opened. The man who hurried in was about five-ten and carrying a good five excess pounds in the belly. His round face held a pleasant if harried smile. Eyes of faded green radiated both fatigue and kindness. He scooped his hand through his short tangle of brown hair.

"I'm so sorry to keep you waiting. We're . . . well, we're short-staffed today, as you know. We didn't have enough time to notify all the staff, the patients, and close today." He sat, wearily. "I think we're all running on sheer nerves. Sorry, I'm Dr Collins, Larry Collins."

"Lieutenant Dallas. I'm sorry for your loss."

"It's incomprehensible. At least a half dozen times today I've started to ask Ava for something. In the six months or so since she's been here, she's become the hub of the practice."

"You're aware she was planning to see Dr Pike last night, socially."

"Yes. We were all invested, a bunch of matchmakers." His lips compressed on the term. "And now . . . Jack couldn't have hurt her, Lieutenant. It's just not possible."

"What time did she leave yesterday?"

"Ah, let me think. I believe she was still here when I left, and that would have been close to five. Yes, yes, because I said good night to her and —" He broke off, looked away, struggled for composure, "— and good luck."

"Where did you go?"

"I went home, and had a drink." He smiled a little. "My last patient of the day was a very, let's say, active and opinionated five-year-old."

"You're a pediatrician?"

"That's right."

Eve nodded, watching him. "I have to ask, it's routine. Is there anyone who can verify your whereabouts from 5p.m. to midnight?"

"My wife. She fixed me the drink, bless her. We had a quiet evening at home as the kids were spending the night with friends."

"All right. Who was here when you left, other than Ava?"

"I'm not entirely sure." He furrowed his brow in thought. "I think Rodney, one of our nurses, and Kiki, a lab tech. I know the waiting room was clear, because I commented on it to Ava. We try to close at five, but realistically it's nearer to six most days."

"Dr Pike? Was he still here?"

"I didn't see him. Of course, he may have been with a patient."

"Thanks for your time. I may have some follow-ups later, but for now, that's it. Would you send either Kiki or Rodney in?"

"I think Rodney's on his lunch break, but I'll see that Kiki's told you're waiting." He rose, walked to the desk where she sat, offered a hand. "Thank you, Lieutenant, for all you're doing."

She got to her feet first so their eyes would be level. She thought of when she might grab a meal, and took his hand. "It's my job."

"All the same." He held her hand, her eyes a moment longer, then released it. "Thank you."

She waited until he'd left the room before she spoke for her recorder. "Note, Dr Lawrence Collins is a sensitive. And one who doesn't mind poking into another's mind without permission."

Hope he enjoyed her thoughts of pepperoni pizza, Eve mused. Then checking the time, pulled out her 'link to check her messages.

She was snarling and steaming before Roarke's message played out. "Son of a bitch!" She tagged him back. "You'd better answer, goddamn it, you'd just better — Stay out of my crime scene," she snapped out when his face came on screen.

"That crime scene is a suite in my hotel."

"Look, pal —"

"You look for a change. One of my people is in custody. Another, I've just been informed, is dead by his own hand. I won't sit and do nothing."

"I'm getting somewhere here, and I'll be in contact with Mira within the hour. She'll have finished the initial exams, and if she gets the results I think I may have enough for a search warrant."

"That's all very well, and good for you. Meanwhile, I've my own line to tug, and at the end of it, you may have enough for arrest warrants."

"You can't just walk into a crime scene and take someone with you. Who the hell is with you?"

"Isis."

There was a long, stunned silence. "You're taking a witch into my crime scene? What the hell's wrong with you? If the two of you compromise —"

"Your sweepers and techs have been through, the scene's been recorded and photographed, evidence removed and logged. You've been over that suite top to bottom yourself. Added to that, goddamn right back at you, I didn't come down in the last shower of rain. I know what's to be done to protect the bleeding scene."

"You both need a nap," Eve heard Isis say, very pleasantly.

"Listen. I'm on the Upper West Side, finishing up interviews with the staff at the health center. I'll be done in about thirty minutes, and can be at the hotel in forty. Wait. Just wait until I get there."

There was another silence, then she saw him nod. "Forty minutes," he said and clicked off.

Eve hissed out a breath, kicked Slone's desk. She might have kicked it a second time, but the door opened.

The woman who came in reeked of Neo-Goth. The black hair, red lips, and the silver hoop through her pierced left brow projected a kind of careless defiance that merged with the tattoo that peeked out from the slope of her breast.

Eve might have considered it all a matter of personal style, along with the snug black top and pants, the chunky black boots, but for the smug gleam in the black-lined eyes.

Weak link, Eve thought, and smiled. "Hello, Kiki."

"I'm swamped." She dumped herself in a chair. "So let's cut to it. I left about five — Ava, the pure and wholesome — was still here, all shiny-eyed about her date with Dr Dull. I lit out, met up with some friends downtown. We hit some clubs, got trashed, hung out, and I got home about two. Is that it?"

"Not quite. I'll need the names and contact information for your friends."

Kiki shrugged, rattled off names and 'link numbers. "You didn't like Ava?"

"Wasn't my type, that's all. Too bad she's dead and all that. Saint Jack probably freaked when she wouldn't put out, and did her." Now those eyes glittered. "But since I wasn't there, I don't know. Ava and I weren't buds, so I got no clue what she was into. You need more, you'll have to catch me later. I'm backed up."

"Thanks for your time."

"Whatev."

Eve waited a few seconds, then walked to the door, stepped out. She saw Kiki at the end of the corridor in an intense conversation with Leah Burke. The moment

70

Leah spotted Eve coming toward them, she squeezed a hand on Kiki's arm to silence her, and started forward. "Lieutenant, can I help you?"

"I'd like to speak to Rodney."

"He's not back from his break." She checked her wrist unit. "He should be only a few more minutes. He's very prompt."

"Okay, I'll take Dr Pratt."

"He's still with a patient. I can't —"

"I'll keep it short. I'm sure we'll all be happy when this is done. Before you interrupt him, what time did you leave last night?"

"Me? Ah, just after five."

"Was Ava still here?"

"No, she'd just left. I, ah, scooted her along, actually, so she could get ready for her date. I closed up last night."

"You were the last to leave?"

"That's right."

"And where did you go?"

"I went home. I, ah, walked home, changed, had some dinner."

"You didn't go out again?"

"No."

"Make or receive any calls, have any visitors?"

"No, it was a quiet night. Lieutenant, I have patients myself."

"Okay. I've only got a couple more staff members, and I'll be out of your hair."

Eve stepped back into Slone's office. Collins, Burke, and Kiki, she thought, were top of her suspect list. She scanned Silas Pratt's data, but he didn't keep her waiting long.

He strode in, a sharply handsome man with an air of confidence. His eyes were a laser blast of blue, and she could admit they gave her a jolt. When he offered his hand she allowed herself to think just that: *Here's a great-looking man with killer eyes.*

He smiled at her. "Lieutenant, I'm Silas Pratt."

Her heart pumped a little harder as he squeezed her hand. She felt the probe of his gaze, and yes, of his power, like heat along her brain. "Have a seat, Dr Pratt," she said and removed her hand from his.

"Can you tell me if you have any leads? Other than Jack. No one who knows him will believe Jack did this to our Ava."

"You've only known him a couple of weeks."

"That's true. Peter recruited him, but I like to think I'm a good judge of character. What they're saying was done to Ava, well, it's monstrous, isn't it? And to someone so young, so vibrant."

Now he did sit, and passed a hand over those potent eyes. "I thought of her almost as a daughter."

"You don't have children. According to your official data."

"No. But it was easy to feel a paternal kind of affection for Ava."

"I don't want to intrude any longer than necessary." And she wanted out, Eve admitted. There was a heat in the room now, a kind of singeing of the air. "When did you leave yesterday?"

"About quarter to five. Ava was getting ready to leave, I remember. Leah was shooing her out. She and Jack — well, you know about all that."

"Yes. Did you approve of that? One of your doctors dating your office manager."

He looked surprised by the question, even bemused. "They were both adults — and frankly, they seemed besotted with each other from the first minute."

"Where did you go when you left?"

"Home to change. My wife and I had a small dinner party last evening. A few friends."

"I apologize, but it's routine. I'll need the names and contact numbers."

"Of course." He smiled at her. "No apology necessary." And he gave her six names. She thanked him, dismissed him. Then added those names to her list of suspects.

CHAPTER
EIGHT

Roarke arranged lunch for himself and Isis in the owner's suite of the hotel, and passed the forty minutes eating food that didn't interest him while making polite small talk with a witch.

"When's the last time you slept?" Isis asked him.

"I suppose it's been about thirty-two hours now. She'll push herself until she drops, you see. Eve."

"And you relax and recreate?"

"More often than she. But no, in this case, in this particular case, I suppose we'll both push. Her time's up, so if you've finished, I'll take you to 606."

"First." She rose, stepped to him, and placed her hand on his head. "No, relax, just for a moment. Clear your mind. You can trust me."

A warm flow, he thought. Not the quick burst of energy that came from popping a booster, but more of a slow, steady build of stamina.

"Better?"

"Thank you, yes."

"It won't last long, but between that and the little you ate, it should get you through. What you need is some rest." She picked up her bag. "I'm ready."

He led her to the elevator.

"You said there's a private elevator that opens into the suite, as well as the doors to the hallways."

"That's right."

"I want to see it from the outside first. I want to go through the door, not through a machine."

"All right. Sixtieth floor," he ordered. "Main bank."

"I'll ask you, whatever happens, not to leave me alone."

"I won't." When the elevator doors opened, Roarke took her hand.

The bloody footprints still walked the carpet. Blood smears marred the walls where Jack had laid his hand for balance. In Roarke's hand, Isis's fingers tensed.

"People think of it as a cliché." She stared at the door where the trail of blood made a six from the middle zero. "But it has power and meaning. It should be cleaned — all of this — with blessed water as soon as possible."

Roarke stepped forward, drew out his master. And Eve strode off the elevator like vengeance.

"Wait. Didn't I tell you to wait?"

"And so I did." Roarke turned to her, his gaze as icy as hers was hot. "You're late."

She put herself between him and the door. "I know who did this. At least I know some of them. I can close this without the mumbo."

"Nice to see you again, Eve."

Eve shifted her gaze to Isis. "No offense. I appreciate you being willing to help, and in fact, have some questions you may be able to answer. You don't have to see what's in there."

"I've already seen some of it, through him and now through you. Seen what's trapped in your minds. But I can't feel unless I go in. I can't feel or see what she saw and felt unless I go in. I might help, I might not, but he needs it."

Isis took Eve's arms so that for a moment, she stood as the link between Eve and Roarke. "You know that."

Eve yanked out her master and turned to the door. "When I say it's done, it's done," she stated.

Roarke slipped the protection charm into her pocket as she unsealed the door.

She stepped in first. "Lights on full." She turned quickly when she heard Isis let out a quick, shuddering breath. But Isis put out a hand, and took another step into the room.

"It reeks still, and will until it's cleansed. No one can stay here until a cleansing. You feel it, do you feel it? This is not the work of a dabbler, not the vile work of one who only seeks blood and death for their own sake. This is power and purpose, and it brought the dark."

"You're going to tell me they called up Satan?"

Isis turned her black eyes on Eve. "I imagine he has more important things to do than answer a summons. But evil can be called, and it can be fed. You can't do what you do and believe otherwise. Or see what you see."

She stared at the pentagram, and the pools and rivers of blood that washed over it. "She doesn't know me, neither in body nor spirit. I need some of her blood. Get that, while I prepare."

She knelt and began taking items from her bag.

Eve said, "Crap," but she stalked off to get swabs from the bathroom amenities.

"I'll need three. Head, heart, hand." Isis set out candles, crystals, herbs.

Though she rolled her eyes, Eve crossed to the pentagram. If she felt a pull when she stepped into it, she willfully pushed it away. She slapped a look toward Roarke as she coated the swabs. "If it ever gets out that I not only allowed but participated in some voodoo bullshit —"

He crouched beside her, took her free hand. "My lips are sealed as long as you want them to be. I owe you for this."

"Damn right you do."

"You're so tired, darling Eve." Before she could evade, he leaned to her, brushed her lips with his.

"There's power there, too," Isis murmured. "We'll need it. Light the candles, please, and stand with me. Together with me while I cast the circle. Hurry. I can't stay here long.

"The power of three in light," she said as Roarke lit the candles. "The power of three in flesh." She took a bag and walked a circle of salt around them. "Order the lights off," she commanded, and when only the candles lit the room, she began to chant in a language Eve didn't recognize.

With a curved knife she turned, like the hand of a compass. Her face glowed; her eyes burned. She placed crystals at the compass points of the circle, then sprinkled herbs into the water she'd poured into a small copper bowl.

Whether it was fatigue or the power of suggestion, Eve felt something cold, cold, brutally cold push against the air.

"It cannot enter what is light. It cannot enter what is bright. And we will not *open!*" Isis threw her hands high, and her biceps quivered with the strain. "I am daughter of the sun, sister of the moon. I am child and servant of the goddess. In this place, at this hour, I call upon her power. Into me, into mine, bring both light and sight divine. Set the murdered spirit free, send her essence into me.

"The power of three, by her blood."

Isis smeared Ava's blood on her forehead, on her breast, on her hand. And falling to her knees, she shook. Her eyes glazed like black glass while her face went white as wax. Horror etched into her features. Both Eve and Roarke dropped down beside her. Her hands grasped theirs, her fingers tightened like wires.

"She's in some sort of trance. We have to get her out."

"We gave our word," Roarke reminded her. "Christ, she's cold as ice."

Isis bowed back until her head nearly touched the floor. And screamed. For one mad moment, Eve imagined she saw a gash open and gush blood from her throat. And when the witch slumped, Eve wasn't certain if she was unconscious or dead.

"Fuck this, we're getting her out of here now."

"Don't leave the circle." Isis's voice was weak, but her eyes fluttered open. "Don't. The red bottle there. I need it, and a little help to sit up."

They eased her up, and taking the bottle, she sipped slowly from it. "It's not an illegal," she said, with both pain and humor in her eyes. "A potion. There's always a price for power."

"You're in pain," Eve said flatly. "We need to get you out of here."

"The circle needs to be closed as it was opened. Properly. Then, yes, we all need to get out of here."

When it was done, and her tools gathered again, Isis leaned on Roarke while Eve resealed the door.

"Can we go back to where we had lunch? I'll tell you what I can tell you, but I want to be away from here."

In the owner's suite, Roarke helped her to the couch, tucked pillows behind her head. "What do you need?" he asked her.

"A really big glass of wine."

"I can get that for you. Lieutenant?"

"Coffee. I understand you're a sensitive," Eve began, "and you believe, strongly believe in your . . . faith."

"You sometimes hear the cries of the dead. Feel their pain, and know their need for you. We're not so far apart." Isis closed her eyes a moment, opening them when Roarke brought her wine. She drank slowly, as she had her potion. "She was a lovely child. I saw some of what they did to her. Not all, I think, not all, but enough. She was inside herself, screaming to get out, but trapped there. There are ways to trap a spirit, with drugs, and other methods. She drank what they gave her, ate, let them touch her. She had no choice. They marked her with a serpent."

Eve thought of the tattoo, said nothing.

"Sex for power. Well, for some of them, it was only sex — the greed for it, the meanness of it. No love, not even lust. Just greed and violence and power. The one they brought her first, not one of them. Trapped as she was. Something there."

Isis touched a hand to her forehead, sipped more wine. "Something light between them," she continued. "Light and new, twisted now when they coupled on the sign. Snuffing out that fragile light with chants and drugs and power until it, too, turned mean. They raped her, took him away and raped her, again and again while she lay unable to fight, to resist. And her trapped spirit screaming, screaming."

"Easy now," Roarke murmured, and took Isis's hand. "Easy."

She nodded, gathered herself again. "They pulled her up, dragged her to the one who leads them. She looked at him. He said her name, and she looked in his eyes when he cut her throat.

"And they fell on her like beasts. I couldn't bear any more. I couldn't bear it."

Eve rose and walked away while Isis wept in absolute silence, while Roarke sat with her, held her hand. She walked to the wide glass doors, yanked them open, and stepped out into the spring air that buzzed like a mad hive from the city.

When Roarke came out, she continued to stare out at the snarls of traffic, the rush of people below. "What am I supposed to do with this?" she demanded. "Go to the

PA and tell him I want to arrest these people because a witch communed with the tragic spirit of the victim?"

"Eve."

He laid a hand on her shoulder, but rather than turn to him, she curled her hands on the rail until they were fists. "I know she didn't bullshit that, okay? I may be cynical, but I'm not stupid. And I'm *sick* at the thought that she saw what she saw. Nobody should. Nobody should have to see that, feel that."

"No one but you?" he asked, and turned her to face him.

She shook her head. "I looked right in the faces of some of the people who did this to that girl. And I looked right in the eyes of one of them, the one I think cut her throat. And for a second — hell, longer — I was scared right down to my guts." She let out a breath. "Now, I'm just pissed off."

He pressed his lips to her forehead. "Then take them down, Lieutenant."

"I damn well will." She put her arms around him first, squeezed. "You pissed me off."

"Same goes. Now, it seems, I'm not. And I just love you."

"I'm still a little pissed." But she tipped her head back, looked into his eyes. "But I love you, too."

Stepping away, she went back to Isis. "Are you steady enough to look at some pictures?"

"Yes."

"Let's hope I don't need your statement, your ID, or . . . the rest of it to take these bastards down. But just in case." Eve pulled a stack of ID photos from her bag, spread them on the coffee table.

"Yes." Shifting to sit up, Isis took another sip of wine. Then, without hesitation, pointed out Ava's murderers.

CHAPTER
NINE

Eve rushed through Central, dodging other cops on the glides on her way to Homicide. The time with Isis had put her behind. She needed to meet with Mira, go over her notes, organize them. Then talk the PA into issuing more than a dozen arrest warrants.

And God, she needed coffee.

She veered toward her bullpen just as Peabody came out.

"I was about to tag you. Grabbing an energy bar first. You want?"

Eve started to decline, the things were disgusting. But they worked. "Yeah. I need to put a couple of things together, then meet with Mira."

At Vending, Peabody plugged in some credits. "You want the Razzmatazz or the Berry Burst?"

"What difference does it make? They're both revolting."

"I kinda like the Berry Burst." As Peabody made the selections, the machine cheerfully congratulated her on her choices, then listed the ingredients and nutritional information. "I checked in with Mira since you were late getting back."

"Ran into stuff. Fill you in. Coffee."

Peabody hiked after Eve to Eve's office. "She said she needed another thirty minutes, that was about five minutes ago. Down-the-hall neighbor at the vic's apartment states the vic never came home after work yesterday. They were supposed to do the girl thing together for the date. Hair, outfit, stuff like that. Ava never showed. Nothing in her apartment to indicate an interest or connection with the occult. EDD's got her electronics."

"She never went back to the apartment because they took her at the clinic." Eve took a bite of the energy bar, washed it down with coffee. She filled Peabody in, and as expected, her partner's eyes went big as planets.

"You — you did like a ritual?"

"You had to be there," Eve muttered.

"No, really happy to pass. Was it scary?"

"The point is, while I'm not sure how much weight the woo-woo might carry in court, Isis fingered every single one of the people on my list. Damn smug is what they are, alibied up. Alibiing each other. Break one, break all. If Mira's got anything solid, we top it off. We've got enough to push for a search warrant on the clinic — and if we push right, on the residences of the staff. Contact the PA. Get them."

"Me? Me?" If she'd just been ordered to run naked through the bullpen, Peabody would've been less stunned. "But you should do it. They listen to you over there. What am I supposed to do?"

"Jesus, Peabody. Sing, dance, shed a goddamn tear. Put the package together and get it done. I've got Mira in fifteen. Go."

She all but shoved Peabody out the door, then closed it. Locked it. She two-pointed the rest of the energy bar into the trash. It wasn't doing the job. She needed five minutes down, she admitted. Just five. She set her wrist unit to alarm, sat at her desk, laid her head down on it, and shut her eyes.

She went straight under.

A sound woke her, a kind of humming. Voices, tinny with distance, tapped on her subconscious. One — young, male — spiked with excitement.

"Look! Flying cars. Look out the window! That is so *cool*."

Eve allowed herself a groan, started to slap at her wrist unit. Opening bleary eyes, she stared groggily at the swirl of luminous blue light, and the man, woman, and child cloaked in its circle. Instinct had her reaching for her weapon even as she registered them — tall man, a lot of gold hair, slim brunette with startled green eyes, and a shaggy-haired boy.

She thought she heard the woman say, "Oops." Then they were gone, and her wrist unit was beeping.

"Okay, with a dream that weird, I need more than five minutes down." She turned off the alarm, scrubbed her hands over her face. After downing the rest of her now lukewarm coffee, she gathered what she needed for Mira.

As she left the office, she shot a frown over her shoulder. Weird, she thought again. The whole damn day was weird.

Mira's admin gave Eve a glare that turned the room into an arctic cave. Knowing the way to Mira lay at the dragon's feet, Eve cut through the bull. "I kicked you, and kicked you hard this morning." She pulled out one of the crime-scene photos. "She's why." And laid it on the desk.

The admin sucked in a breath, held it, let it out slowly. "I see. Yes. She's waiting for you, Lieutenant."

"Thanks." Eve picked up the photo and walked into Mira's office.

Mira wasn't at her desk but standing at the window, her back to the room. She looked smaller somehow, Eve thought. Almost delicate in her quiet lavender suit.

"Dr Mira."

"Yes. Such a lovely day. Sometimes you need to remember the world is full of lovely days. You've had a very long one, haven't you?"

"It's got a ways to go yet."

Mira turned. Her sable hair curled around her pretty face, but her eyes looked tired and troubled. "Where do you want me to begin?"

"I know what happened, and I know who's responsible. At least the main players. I need to know what was done to Jackson Pike and Mika Nakamura, how it was done, and who did it. What was done to them was also done to the desk clerk at the hotel, and he bashed his own brains out with a hammer. So I need to know if it was done to anyone else."

Rather than sit in one of her cozy scoop chairs as was her habit, Mira continued to stand. "First, the toxicology screening showed a combination of drugs in their systems. I have that list for you. Both had a hallucinogenic in their bloodstream and a drug we sometimes use to control patients with violent tendencies. As you know, both Pike and the victim were also given sexual drugs."

"Would that explain the headaches, the memory blanks?"

"The combination would likely result in a kind of chemical hangover, but no, not the violent pain. There may be blank spots as well, but again, no, that's not my conclusion."

She did sit now. "The drugs were used to begin a process, and to enhance it."

"They've been hypnotized."

"You're ahead of me."

"No, but I'm hoping we're on pace. At least two of the suspects are sensitives. They took a pass at me. Since I've dealt with a homicidal psychic before, I used the same method to block them, to steer them away. One of them, Silas Pratt, he's . . . Look, I know you've got a daughter who's Wiccan, and I get there are theories and faiths and even documentation, studies, blah, blah. I'm not big on that. But this guy?"

It went against the grain to admit it. "He's got a punch," Eve told her.

"You don't want to use the word 'power'."

"It doesn't take power to load people up with drugs, or to hypnotize them. It's a technique. You use it." She stuffed her hands in her pockets and began to pace. "One of these bastards is Mika's kid's doctor. She took the kid in for a standard check-up three weeks ago. So, we theorize Pratt hypnotizes her. Maybe they slip her something first to make her more susceptible, but he takes her under, and gives her the assignment. Posthypnotic suggestion, right?"

"Yes."

"It needs a trigger — something she sees, hears. Easy enough to take care of that while she's on her way to work, maybe give her a booster shot. She goes in, shuts down the cameras. They had to get to the desk clerk. We'll find the intersect there, but they turned him on like a damn droid. They waltz Pike and the victim right in. They go along like puppies. They're loaded by then, and under . . ."

"A spell?"

"If that's the word. Pike's left as patsy, with that trigger still cocked in his head. The pain's impossible, and trying to remember takes it up to excruciating."

"I believe if you hadn't gotten them to me, into a controlled, medical environment when you did, they'd have ended it as the desk clerk did. I've had to use that pain to try to get to the trigger. It's . . . difficult."

Understanding, Eve moved to Mira's AutoChef. "What's that tea you're always drinking?"

Mira managed a smile. "It varies. I think jasmine would be nice. Thank you."

Eve programmed a cup, brought it to Mira, took a seat. "You're not hurting them. You know that. The one who cocked the trigger is."

"They, both of them, begged me to kill them." Mira sipped the tea, then eased wearily back in the chair.

"It's taken hours for me to find the right method to dial the pain down. Not turn it off, not yet, but lower it from inhuman to hideous. Enough that Jack remembered a little. He remembered that Dr Pratt called him into his office at the end of the day. He's not sure of the time, it's cloudy, but thinks it was after his last patient. Pratt gave him a cup of coffee, and after he drank it, it's more jumbled. He remembers being in a limo with Collins and Ava. He thinks there were more. I recorded everything, of course. He remembers having sex with Ava."

"Does he remember the murder?"

Her eyes troubled, Mira shook her head. "He's suppressing. Even without the trigger, his mind's not ready to go there. He next remembers waking in a bed, covered with blood, and a woman he called Leah sitting beside him, crying."

"Leah Burke. Good, that's good. I can break her, and she'll take them all down with her."

"It wasn't just a young woman killed in that suite, Eve. Parts of the two people I have sedated and restrained for their own safety were murdered in there. When I find the way to remove the trigger and they remember what was done, their part in it however unwilling, they'll never be the same."

"You'll help them deal with it, or find someone who'll help them deal with it. It's what you do."

"Take them down, Eve. Take them down hard. When I can tell Mika and Jack that's been done, we can start on the healing."

In all the time they'd worked together, Mira had never asked. Eve rose. "Like you said, it's a lovely day. Before it's over, they'll be down."

As she walked out, Eve whipped out her communicator to contact Peabody. "Search warrants?"

"It's looking good on the clinic. I just need to —"

"Put a hold on it. We've got a wit who puts Leah Burke in Suite 606. We're bringing her in. Book an interview room."

"You want me to have her picked up?"

"Here's how it goes. Two uniforms at her door. If she's not home yet, I need to know ASAP. She's not under arrest, and she's not to be read her rights. Got that?"

"Got it."

"She's needed down here for further questioning. That's all they know. She's not to be permitted to contact anyone. She's not under arrest. I'll finish up with the search warrants."

Eve was still listing the names for the APA when she approached Homicide. What sounded like a small riot had her quickening her steps.

Then she smelled the pizza. "Yeah, I mean even the house in the Caribbean. I've got goddamn probable cause right down the line. I've got witness statements, and within two hours I'm going to hand you a confession on a goddamn platter that will take down every son of a bitch on the list I just gave you. They're going to have hoodoo voodoo crap tucked away," Eve said meeting Roarke's eyes as she stepped into the bullpen. "Because they believe it. A dozen blades were used on the vic. We're going to find some, most, or all of them."

She clicked off. "Figured you'd be back around after you got your witch home."

"You haven't eaten." He picked up a box of pizza while her men swarmed like ants over the five others he'd brought in. "Eat now."

She grabbed a slice, chomped a huge bite. "Oh. God. Good." She swallowed, took another. "I got them."

"I can see that. Can I watch?"

She took the tube of Pepsi he offered, guzzled. "It's a good bribe. Take Observation."

CHAPTER
TEN

Revived and revved, Eve stood with Roarke in Observation and watched Leah pace the interview room in her smart suit.

"She's already sweating. Ten minutes in, and she's already sweating. She's scared and guilty, and the doctors aren't here to tell her what to do, what to say."

"Why her? Out of all of them?"

"She cried." She glanced over as Mira came in.

"Word's out that you have one of them in," Mira said. "I wanted to see for myself."

"I haven't arrested her yet. Listen, I'm going to ask you not to turn on the audio until I give you the go. Actually, I'm not asking. I've got to get started."

"Will I be able to see Mika?" Roarke asked Mira after Eve stepped out.

"Not yet. She's comfortable for the moment. I've spoken with her husband."

"So have I. Is there anything I can do for her?"

"There will be." Mira laid a hand over Roarke's, and watched Eve enter Interview. "What she's going to say needs to be off the record. At least for my ears."

"Do you object?"

"No." Mira stared at Leah Burke through the glass. "No, I don't."

Inside, Leah spun toward Eve. "I demand to know why I was brought here, why I'm being treated this way. I have rights. I have —"

"Shut the fuck up. You've got nothing here until I give it to you. Sit down."

The words, the tone, had Leah's whole body recoiling. "I will not —"

"I'll put you down, bitch. Believe it."

The threat, so hot and hard in Eve's eyes, had Leah sitting at the small table. "You'll lose your badge." But her voice trembled, just a little. "Worse. There are laws."

Eve slammed both fists on the table, hard enough to have Leah covering her face in defense. "Laws? I bet you were thinking about *laws* when Ava Marsterson was being hacked to death. Jack remembers, Leah." She leaned close, snapped her fingers in front of Leah's face. "Boom. Spell broken. You've got one shot. One, then I move on to the next. But I'll hurt you first."

"You can't touch me. You can't put your hands on me. I want —"

"I know how to hurt you so it won't show." Eve let the heat burn in her eyes as she circled the table. "Your word against mine. Decorated cop against murder suspect. Guess who they'll believe? I haven't put this on record. I haven't read you your rights. And we're all alone here, Leah. One shot once I turn on the record. You don't take it, I move to Kiki or Rodney, to Larry's wife, and down the line — and you go back to a cage blubbering with the pain.

"Everybody gets one shot. Take it, I deal down to Murder Two. You'll do life, but you'll do it on planet. Pass? And you'll find out what hell really is because you'll be in some concrete cage in an off-planet penal colony where I will personally see that word gets out you fucked with tiny little children. Do you know what cons like to do to people who fuck with tiny little children?"

"I've never touched a child —"

"I'll lie." Eve grinned. "And I'll love it. One shot, and if you so much as *think* lawyer, it's done. You only get the chance because Jack's soft-hearted enough to think you feel real bad about what happened. Me? I'm hoping you pass so I can look forward to getting the reports on how many inventive ways the other cons and the guards rape you over the next, oh, fifty years."

She came around the table, whispered in Leah's ear. "They find ways to get sharp, ugly tools into those cages, Leah. They'll slice and dice you, let them stitch you up again just so they can slice and dice some more. The more you beg, the more they'll enjoy it."

She watched tears plop on Leah's trembling hands, on the rough surface of the table. And thinking of Ava, felt no pity. "She trusted you, you bitch."

"Please. Oh, please."

"Screw you." Eve walked to the door, stepped out. She took a deep breath, signaled Peabody. "Let's do it." Walking back in, she nodded toward the observation glass. "Record on. Dallas, Lieutenant Eve —"

"Please, please. I'll tell you everything."

"Hey, great." Eve slid into her chair, composed and easy. "Let's just get everything on record first, and read you your rights."

When she'd finished, she nodded to Leah. "What do you want to tell us, Ms Burke?"

"I didn't know it would be like that. I swear, I swear I didn't know."

"Like what?"

"So much blood. I never thought they would really kill her."

"Be more specific."

"I thought it would be a symbolic death."

"Bullshit." Eve leaned back in her chair with the warning in her eyes clear. *Lie, and your one shot dies.* "You knew exactly what was going to happen, and when it did, you couldn't handle it. If you want me to go to the PA and say you came in, you confessed, you gave the details and feel remorse, don't bullshit me. Did you participate in the ritual murder of Ava Marsterson?"

"Yes. I didn't understand. Believe me, I didn't understand. I thought I did, but . . . She didn't accept, and neither did Jack. Not like Silas said they would."

"Silas Pratt participated in the murder of Ava Marsterson?"

"He cut her throat. She just stood there, and he cut her throat, and the blood gushed out of her. She didn't accept. She didn't know what was happening, so how could she accept?"

"Accept what?"

"Her sacrifice. That she would be the gift."

"Whose gift?"

"The gift from us to the prince. To Lucifer."

"How long have you been a satanist?"

"I am *not* a satanist. I am a disciple of the One."

Eve gave it a moment, unsure if she was amused or irritated by the obvious insult in Leah's voice. "Okay. And does the One demand the murder of innocents?"

"Your God murdered my child." Leah's hands balled into fists, beat lightly on the table. "He took her, and what had she ever done? She was just a baby. I found my way back. I found my strength and my purpose."

"Silas Pratt showed you the way back."

"He's a great man. You'll never understand. A man of power. You'll never hold him with your pitiful laws and your bars."

"But he lied to you, this great man, this man of power," Peabody put in. "He lied to you about Ava and Jack."

"No, I think . . . No, he wouldn't lie. I think he miscalculated, that's all. She just wasn't ready. Wasn't as strong as Silas thought. Or maybe it's me. Maybe I'm weak. I couldn't stand what they did to her."

"Tell me who they are. Every name of everyone who was in Suite 606."

"Silas and his wife, Ola. Larry — Dr Collins, and his wife, Bria." In a dull, empty voice, she gave Eve a dozen names in addition to her own. "And Ava and Jack."

"Dr Slone?"

"No. Peter and the others from the clinic who weren't there aren't disciples or priests. It's important,

Silas thinks, that there are those who aren't part of us — and to know who is open to our faith, and who would be closed. Everyone who is of our group attended. It was an important ritual, a celebration."

"A celebration?"

"Yes. It was Silas's birthday."

"I've seen his records. It wasn't his birthday."

"His date of rebirth in the One."

"Right." Eve sat back again. "Why Ava and Jack?"

"Ava was the gift. Silas recognized her as such the day she came in to interview for the position. And Jack . . . the sexual energy between them would be a vital element to the ritual."

"Why that room?"

"We'd considered other venues, but . . . A palace, it seemed right. And Larry's connection to the head of security gave us the way in. I'm only a disciple. I don't plan." She folded her hands now, bowed her head. "I follow."

"You followed them into that suite. But first you helped drug Ava and Jack at the clinic."

"We gave them what would open them to the coming ritual, what would help them accept, and embrace Silas's power."

"He used hypnosis, Leah, on top of hallucinogens."

Tears continued to gather and spill. "You don't understand. You're closed."

"Fine. You used chemicals to open Ava and Jack, without their knowledge or permission."

"Yes, but —"

"And once they were under that influence, you took them to the hotel. Correct?"

"Yes."

"There, Mika Nakamura and Brian Trosky had also been drugged, and *embraced* by Silas's power. That power caused them to shut down the security cameras to the lobby, and to the elevators for the sixtieth floor. It also, as had been done to Jack, caused them to forget what had been done, or suffer pain."

"The pain is only if they refuse to accept, only to help them —"

"Inside the room, you ate and you drank, you engaged in sexual activity."

Color flushed into her cheeks. It was amazing, Eve mused, what embarrassed murderers.

"Sex is an offering."

"Ava didn't offer, did she? After you'd feasted and stoked up, painted your pentagram, lit your candles, said whatever it is you people say, you stretched out a drugged, helpless, naked woman on the floor, and told a drugged, helpless man to have at her. He cared for her. They cared for each other, isn't that true?"

"Yes, yes, but —"

"And when he finished what he'd have never done of his own will, the rest of you raped her."

"Yes." Tears rolled down her cheeks. "Everyone was required to take from the gift, and to give of ourselves. But I felt . . ."

"What?"

"Cold. So cold. Not the heat, not the fire, but ice. I heard her screaming in my head. I swear I *heard* her."

She covered her face with her hands. "But no one would listen. They pulled her to her feet. Kiki and Rodney. Silas stepped into the circle, and the cold, the cold was terrible. Her screaming was like spikes in my head. But no one heard her. He slashed her throat, and her blood sprayed all over him. Everyone rushed forward when she fell to take more blood, to make more blood. Jack passed out, so they coated him with her blood. They took him upstairs, left him in bed while they finished with her. Larry told me to go up, to take one of the knives and put it in Jack's hand, and to give him another round of drugs so he'd overdose."

"The plan was to kill Jack, leave him behind, so it looked as if he'd killed Ava."

"Yes. Yes. But I couldn't. I couldn't give him more. Her blood was on my hands, and I could hear her screaming." She laid down her head and wept.

"Give her five minutes to pull it together," Eve told Peabody. "The charge is Murder in the Second, two counts," she added, thinking of Trosky. "Additional charges are kidnapping, two counts, rape, inducing chemicals without consent or knowledge, including illegals. Have her booked and bolted. I'm going to go get us a shitload of warrants."

Lack of sleep didn't put a hitch in Eve's stride as she walked to Silas Pratt's front door. Big, fancy house, she noted. Well, he'd seen the last of that. The droid that answered looked down its nose. "Dr and Mrs Pratt are unavailable at this time. Please leave your name and state your business, and —"

He didn't get any further as Eve shoved him aside. "Shut that thing down," she ordered the uniforms that trailed after her and Peabody. She walked into the spacious living area where the doctor and his wife were sipping martinis.

"Exactly what is the meaning of this?" Silas demanded as he surged to his feet.

"Deal with the woman, Peabody. He's mine. Silas Pratt, you're under arrest. The charges are Murder in the First Degree in the death of Ava Marsterson, a human being. Murder in the First Degree in the death of —"

"This is absurd. You're absurd."

Eve felt that *punch* of his, accepted the ice that coated her belly. Even welcomed it. "Don't interrupt. Resist, by all means, because I'd love to spend the next several minutes kicking your ass. Jesus, Peabody, can't you shut her up?"

"She's a screamer," Peabody said cheerfully as she passed the hysterical Ola to waiting uniforms.

"Now where was I? Oh yeah, the death of Brian Trosky, another human being. We've got kidnapping charges, illegals, fraud, medical abuse, and just for fun, destruction of property. You guys seriously trashed that suite. You have the right to remain silent," she began.

"You can go to hell."

"Thanks, but New York's close enough for me." She grabbed one of his arms to pull it behind his back as she read him the rest of the Revised Miranda. When he tried to shake her off, she gave herself the pleasure of slamming the heel of her boot into his instep. He

100

cursed at her, snarled at her as she clapped the restraints to his wrist. "What is that, Latin? Greek? Or is it just all made up?"

He struggled as she frog-marched him across the room, which, she thought, it could be argued was the reason his head smacked into the doorjamb. "Gee, I bet you're going to have a headache now. Cut it out, before you hurt yourself."

"I'll drink your blood from a silver cup."

"That's just disgusting." She moved her mouth close to his ear. "You don't have any power here, asshole. Getting arrested, dragged out of your fancy house in front of your fancy neighbors, and hey, look, it's Channel 75." She beamed, pleased her heads-up to her contact there had brought the media. "Nothing like humiliation to water down power. I bet even the devil himself's embarrassed."

She muscled him into the back of the police car. She fixed dark glasses over his head, over his eyes. "Remember he's a sensitive," she told the cops she'd put in charge. "He goes straight into isolation."

She slammed the door, put her hands on her hips. "Go home, Peabody," she said when her partner stepped beside her and yawned until her jaw cracked. "Get some sleep."

"I am so on that. Some day, huh?"

"Yeah, some day." Eve stood where she was, watched Roarke come to her. Gosh, she thought, pretty. And realized sleep deprivation had gooed up her brain.

"I imagine this arrest will be playing on screen for some time."

"That's entertainment." Eve gave him a quick smile.

"Please tell me you're not going to make all the other arrests personally, then deal with the ensuing paperwork tonight."

"Nah, I just wanted this one, 'specially. I delegated, and the paperwork'll wait till morning. I'm pretty close to falling on my face."

He put his arms around her, amused that she was tired enough not to resist even though some of the media remained. "I want to go home, sleep with my wife. For days."

"Settle for eight straight hours?"

"Deal."

With their arms around each other's waist they walked to the car. Roarke got behind the wheel; Eve slid into the passenger's seat. And, he noted, got started on that eight hours immediately.

Epilogue

Jack sat up in bed when Eve entered his treatment room. He was pale, and bruises of fatigue dogged his eyes. No doubt she'd had a more restful night than he had. "Doctor?" he began.

"Lieutenant. Lieutenant Dallas. Do you remember me?"

He stared through her for a moment. "Yes. I remember." He held up a hand, a signal to wait. And shutting his eyes, breathed. "I remember. You were at the hotel, but not, not in that room. And you were talking to me in another room. The police station. Am I under arrest?"

"No, Jack. I know you're working with Dr Mira. She says you're better than you were, and you'll be better yet."

"The drugs are out of my system. It helps. The headaches . . . it's not as bad. Ava's dead. I was there." The words trembled out. Once more he closed his eyes, breathed. "I was there. I raped her."

"No, you didn't. They used you both. You're a doctor, Jack. I know Mira told you what they'd put in you, and you know what those chemicals can do. You

103

were drugged, put under hypnosis. Kidnapped. Nothing that happened was your fault or responsibility. You were a victim."

"I'm alive. She's not."

"I know. That's hard. You're afraid to remember, afraid to ask if you used the knife you had in your hand."

His eyes welled, and tears leaked out. "How can I live with that? Whatever they put in me, whatever they did, how can I live with that?"

"You don't have to. You didn't use the knife. I have a number of statements from people who were there, who were involved. Every one of them says you passed out. They put the knife in your hand when you were upstairs, unconscious."

"The blood. Her blood."

"They put it on you. You were supposed to die, holding the knife, covered in her blood. There would have been questions, sure, a lot of questions. Who else was with you. They had two other people they believed would be dead who'd be tied in. One of them is dead, Jack — he didn't do anything, and he's dead. Another is across the hall in a room like this, struggling to deal with what happened. They drugged her, used her. Do you blame her for Ava?"

"No. God."

"Why blame yourself?"

"I couldn't get out. I couldn't get *out* of . . . myself, and help her. Even when I heard her screaming. In my head."

"Thirteen people killed Ava. You weren't one of them. Because you lived, we found them. Every one of them is locked up. Every one of them is going to pay. You lived, and you found me, Jack. I was in suite 606. I saw what was done to her. I had her blood on my hands. She was in my head, too, Jack. I'm telling you, she doesn't blame you. She doesn't want you to carry this."

He put out a hand, took hers. "They're going to pay?"

"Every goddamn one."

"Thank you."

She stepped out, and watched through the observation window as Roarke leaned over and kissed Mika on the brow.

"How is she?" she asked when he came out.

"Better. Better than I'd hoped, really. Mira said she has a strong mind. How about your Jack?"

"He'll get there."

Roarke took her hand. "Another long day, Lieutenant, with all your interrogations and reports and media conferences."

"You had one, too, I imagine, making up for the time lost yesterday. Buying up wide chunks of the universe takes it out of a guy."

"Yet I feel surprisingly . . . fresh."

"Good, because I want to go home and sleep with my husband — in a much more active sense than last night." She let him keep her hand as they walked away from the treatment rooms. "You know, I found this little bag full of stones and flowery things in the pocket of the jacket I had on yesterday. How do you suppose that got there?"

"Hmm. Magic?"

She gave him a shoulder bump and let it go. As far as she was concerned, the only magic she'd ever need was the good strong grip of his hand in hers.

MISSING IN DEATH

CHAPTER
ONE

On a day kissed gently by summer, three thousand, seven hundred and sixty-one passengers cruised the New York Harbor on the Staten Island Ferry. Two of them had murder on their minds.

The other three thousand, seven hundred and fifty-nine aboard the bright orange ferry christened the *Hillary Rodham Clinton* were simply along for the ride. Most were tourists who happily took their vids and snaps of the retreating Manhattan skyline or that iconic symbol of freedom, the Statue of Liberty.

Even in 2060, nearly two centuries after she'd first greeted hopeful immigrants to a new world, nobody beat "The Lady".

Those who jockeyed for the best views munched on soy chips, sucked down tubes of soft drinks from the snack bars while the ferry chugged placidly along on calm waters under baby blue skies.

With the bold sun streaming, the scent of sunscreen mixed with the scent of water, many jammed the decks for the duration of the twenty-five-minute ride from Lower Manhattan to Staten Island. A turbo would have taken half the time, but the ferry wasn't about expediency. It was about tradition.

Most planned to get off at St George, jam the terminal, then simply load back on again to complete the round trip. It was free, it was summer, it was a pretty way to spend an hour.

Some midday commuters, eschewing the bridges, the turbos, or the air trams, sat inside, out of the biggest crowds, and passed the time with their PPCs or 'links.

Summer meant more kids. Babies cried or slept, toddlers whined or giggled, and parents sought to distract the bored or fractious by pointing out the grand lady or a passing boat.

For Carolee Grogan of Springfield, Missouri, the ferry ride checked off another item on her Must Do list on the family vacation she'd lobbied for. Other Must Dos included the top of the Empire State Building, the Central Park Zoo, the Museum of Natural History, St Pat's, the Metropolitan Museum of Art (though she wasn't sure she'd successfully harangue her husband and ten- and seven-year-old sons into that one), Ellis Island, Memorial Park, a Broadway show — she didn't care which one — and shopping on Fifth Avenue.

In the spirit of fairness, she'd added on a ball game at Yankee Stadium, and fully accepted she would have to wander the cathedral of Tiffany's alone while her gang hit the video heaven of Times Square.

At forty-three, Carolee was living a long-cherished dream. She'd finally pushed, shoved and nagged her husband east of the Mississippi.

Could Europe be far behind?

When she started to take a snapshot of her "boys", as she called Steve and their sons, a man standing nearby offered to take one of the whole family. Carolee happily turned over her camera, posed with her boys with the dignified lady of liberty behind them.

"See." She gave her husband an elbow poke as they went back to looking out at the water. "He was nice. Not all New Yorkers are rude and nasty."

"Carolee, he was a tourist, just like us. He's probably from Toledo or somewhere." But he smiled when he said it. It was more fun to yank her chain than to admit he was having a pretty good time.

"I'm going to ask him."

Steve only shook his head as his wife walked over to chat up the picture taker. It was so Carolee. She could — and did — talk to anyone anywhere about anything.

When she came back she offered Steve a smug smile. "He's from Maryland, *but*," she added with a quick finger jab, "he's lived in New York for almost ten years. He's going over to Staten Island to visit his daughter. She just had a baby. A girl. His wife's been staying with them the past few days to help out, and she's meeting him at the terminal. It's their first grandchild."

"Did you find out how long he's been married, where and how he met his wife, who he voted for in the last election?"

She laughed and gave Steve another poke.

"I'm thirsty."

She glanced down at her youngest. "You know, me too. Why don't you and I go get some drinks for everybody." She grabbed his hand and snaked her way through the people crowded on deck. "Are you having a good time, Pete?"

"It's pretty neat, but I really want to go see the penguins."

"Tomorrow, first thing."

"Can we get a soy dog?"

"Where are you putting them? You had one an hour ago."

"They smell good."

Vacation meant indulgence, she decided. "Soy dogs it is."

"But I have to pee."

"Okay." As a veteran mother, she'd scoped out the restrooms when they'd boarded the ferry. Now she detoured to steer them toward the nearest facilities.

And, of course, since Pete mentioned it, now *she* had to pee. She pointed toward the men's room. "If you get out first, you stand right here. You remember what the ferry staff looks like, the uniforms? If you need help, go right to one of them."

"Mom, I'm just going to pee."

"Well, me, too. You wait for me *here* if you get out first."

She watched him go in, knowing full well he rolled his eyes the minute his back was to her. It amused her as she turned toward the women's room.

And saw the Out of Order sign.

"Shoot."

She weighed her options. Hold it until Pete came out, then hold it some more while they got the dogs and drinks — because he'd whine and sulk otherwise — then make her way to the other restroom.

Or . . . maybe she could just peek in. Surely not all the stalls were out of order. She only needed one.

She pushed open the door, hurried in. She didn't want to leave Pete alone for long.

She made the turn at the line of sinks, her mind on getting the provisions and squeezing back to the rail to watch Staten Island come into view.

She stopped dead, her limbs frozen in shock.

Blood, she thought, could only think, so much blood. The woman on the floor seemed bathed in it.

The man standing over the body held a still-dripping knife in one hand and a stunner in the other.

"I'm sorry," he said — and, to her shocked mind, sounded sincere.

Even as Carolee sucked in the air to scream, took the first stumbling step back, he triggered the stunner.

"Really very sorry," he said as Carolee fell to the floor.

Racing across New York Harbor in a turbo wasn't how Lieutenant Eve Dallas expected to spend her afternoon. She'd played second lead that morning to her partner's primary role in the unfortunate demise of Vickie Trendor, the third wife of the unrepentant Alan Trendor, who'd smashed her skull with an inferior bottle of California chardonnay.

According to the new widower, it wasn't accurate to say he'd bashed her brains out when she simply hadn't had any brains to begin with.

While the prosecutor and the counsel for the defense hammered out a plea arrangement, Eve had made a dent in her paperwork, discussed strategy with two of her detectives on an ongoing case and congratulated another on closing one.

A pretty good day, in her estimation.

Now, she and Peabody, her partner, were speeding across the water in a boat she judged to be about the size of a surfboard toward the orange hulk of a ferry stalled halfway between Manhattan and Staten Island.

"This is absolutely mag!" Peabody stood near the bow, her square-jawed face lifted to the wind, her short, flippy hair flying.

"Why?"

"Jeez, Dallas!" Peabody lowered her shades down her nose, exposing delighted brown eyes. "We're getting a boat ride. We're on the water. Half the time you can forget Manhattan's an island."

"That's what I like about it. Out here, it makes you wonder, how come it doesn't sink? All that weight — the buildings, the streets, the people. It should go down like a stone."

"Come on." With a laugh, Peabody pushed her shades back in place. "Statue of Liberty," she pointed out. "She's the best."

Eve wouldn't argue. She'd come close to dying inside the landmark, fighting radical terrorists bent on blowing it up. Even now, she could look at its lines, its grandeur, and see her husband, bleeding, clinging to a ledge outside the proud face.

They'd survived that one, she mused, and Roarke had defused the bomb, saved the day. Symbols mattered, and because they'd fought and bled, people could chug by on the ferry every day and snap their pictures of freedom.

That was fine, that was the job. What she didn't get was why Homicide had to zip off the island because the Department of Transportation cops couldn't find a passenger.

Blood all over a bathroom and a missing woman. Interesting, sure, she decided, but not really her turf. In fact, it wasn't turf at all. It was water. It was a big orange boat on the water.

Why didn't boats sink? The errant thought reminded her that sometimes they did, and she decided not to dwell on it.

When the turbo approached that big orange boat, she noted people ranged along the rail on the tiers of decks. Some of them waved.

Beside her, Peabody waved back.

"Cut it out," Eve ordered.

"Sorry. It's knee-jerk. Looks like DOT sent out backup," she commented, nodding toward the turbos at the base of the ferry with the Department of Transportation logo emblazoned on the hull. "I hope she didn't fall over. Or jump. But somebody would notice that, right?"

"More likely she wandered off from the passenger areas, got lost and is currently trying to wander back."

"Blood," Peabody reminded her, and Eve shrugged.

"Let's just wait and see."

That, too, was part of the job — the waiting and seeing. She'd been a cop for a dozen years and knew the dangers of jumping to conclusions.

She shifted her weight as the turbo slowed, bracing on long legs while she scanned the rails, the faces, the open areas. Her short hair fluttered around her face while those eyes — golden brown, long and cop-flat — studied what might or might not be a crime scene.

When the turbo was secured, she stepped off.

She judged the man who stepped forward to offer his hand as late twenties. He wore the casual summer khakis and light blue shirt with its DOT emblem well. Sun-streaked hair waved around a face tanned by sun or design. Pale green eyes contrasted with the deeper tone, and added an intensity.

"Lieutenant, Detective, I'm Inspector Warren. I'm glad you're here."

"You haven't located your passenger, Inspector?"

"No. A search is still under way." He gestured for them to walk with him. "We've added a dozen officers to the DOT crew aboard to complete the search, and to secure the area where the missing woman was last seen."

They started up a set of stairs.

"How many passengers aboard?"

"The ticker counted three thousand, seven hundred and sixty-one boarding at Whitehall."

"Inspector, it wouldn't be procedure to call Homicide on a missing passenger."

"No, but none of this is hitting SOP. I have to tell you, Lieutenant, it doesn't make sense." He took the next set of stairs, glancing over at the people hugging the rail. "I don't mind admitting, this situation is above

116

my pay grade. And right now, most of the passengers are being patient. It's mostly tourists, and this is kind of an adventure. But if we hold the ferry here much longer, it's not going to be pretty."

Eve stepped onto the next deck where DOT officials had cordoned off a path. "Why don't you give me a rundown, Inspector?"

"The missing woman is Carolee Grogan, tourist from Missouri, on board with her husband and two sons. Age forty-three. I've got her description and a photo taken aboard this afternoon. She and her youngest went to get drinks, hit the Johns first. He went into the men's, and she was going into the women's. Told him to wait for her right outside if he got out first. He waited, and she didn't come out."

Warren paused outside the restroom area, nodded to another DOT official on the women's room door. "Nobody else went in or out either. After a few minutes, he called her on his 'link. She didn't answer. He called his father, and the father and the other son came over. The father, Steven Grogan, asked a woman — ah, Sara Hunning — if she'd go in and check on his wife."

Warren opened the door. "And this is what she found inside."

Eve stepped in behind Warren. She smelled the blood immediately. A homicide cop gets a nose for it. It soured the citrusy/sterilized odor of the air in the black-and-white room with its steel sinks, and around the dividing wall, the white-doored stalls.

It washed over the floor, a spreading dark pool that snaked in trails across the white, slashed over the stall doors, the opposing wall, like abstract graffiti.

"If that's Grogan's," Eve said, "you're not looking for a missing passenger. You're looking for a dead one."

CHAPTER
TWO

"Record on, Peabody." Eve switched on her own. "Dallas, Lieutenant Eve; Peabody, Detective Delia; Warren, DOT Inspector . . ."

"Jake," he supplied.

"On scene aboard Staten Island Ferry."

"It's the *Hillary Rodham Clinton*," he added. "Second deck, port side, women's restroom."

She cocked a brow, nodded. "Responding to report of missing passenger, Grogan, Carolee, last seen entering this area. Peabody, get a sample of the blood. We'll need to make sure it's human, then type it."

She opened the field kit she hadn't fully believed she'd need for Seal-It. "How many people have been in and out of here since Grogan was missed?"

"Since I've been on board, just me. Prior, to the best of my knowledge, Sara Hunning, Steven Grogan and two ferry officers on board."

"There's an Out of Order sign on the door."

"Yeah."

"But she came in anyway."

"Nobody we've spoken to can absolutely confirm. She told the kid she was going in."

Sealed, Eve stepped into the first of the four stalls, waved a hand over the sensor. The toilet flushed efficiently. She repeated the gesture in the other three stalls, with the same results.

"Appears to be in order."

"It's human," Peabody told her, holding up her gauge. "Type A Negative."

"Some smears, but no drag marks," Eve murmured. She gestured toward a narrow utility closet. "Who opened that?"

"I did," Jake told her. "On the chance she — or her body — was in there. It was locked."

"There's only one way in and out." Peabody walked around to the sink area. "No windows. If that's Carolee Grogan's blood, she didn't stand up and walk out of here."

Eve stood at the edge of the blood pool. "How do you get a dead body out of a public restroom, on a ferry in the middle of the harbor, under the noses of more than three thousand people? And why the hell don't you leave it where it dropped in the first place?"

"It's not an answer to that," Jake began, "but this is a tourist boat. It doesn't carry any vehicles, has extra concession areas. People tend to hug the rails and look out, or hang in a concession and snack as they watch out the windows. Still, it'd take a lot of luck and enormous *cojones* to cart a bleeding body along the deck."

"Balls maybe, but nobody's got that kind of luck. I'll need this room sealed, Inspector. And I want to talk to the missing woman's family, and the witness. Peabody, let's get the sweepers out here. I want every inch of this room covered."

Eve considered Jake's foresight in having the Grogan family sequestered in one of the canteens solid. It kept them away from other passengers, gave them seats, and access to food and drink. That, she assumed, had kept the kids calm.

Calm enough, she noted, for the smaller of the two boys to curl on the narrow seat of the booth with his head in his father's lap.

The man continued to stroke the boy's hair, and his face was both pale and frightened when Eve crossed to him.

"Mr Grogan, I'm Lieutenant Dallas, with the New York City Police and Security Department. This is Detective Peabody."

"You found her. You found Carolee. She's —"

"We haven't yet located your wife."

"She told me to wait." The boy with his head on Steve's lap opened his eyes. "I did. But she didn't come back."

"Did you see her go into the other bathroom?"

"Nuh-uh, but she said she was gonna, and then we were going to get dogs and drinks. And she gave me the routine."

"Routine?"

He sat up, but leaned against his father's side. "How I had to wait *right* there, and how if I needed anything, I was supposed to get one of the guys who work on the boat. The uniform guys."

"Okay. Then you went into the men's bathroom."

"It was only for a minute. I just had to . . . you know. Then I came out and waited like she said. It *always* takes girls longer. But it was really long, and I was thirsty. I used my 'link." He slid his eyes toward his father. "We're only allowed to use them if it's really important, but I was thirsty."

"It's okay, Pete. She didn't answer, so Pete tagged me, and Will and I headed back to where he was waiting. They'd been gone at least ten minutes by then. There was the Out of Order sign on the door, so I thought she might've used another restroom. Except she wouldn't. She wouldn't have left Pete. So I asked this woman if she'd just take a look inside. And then . . ."

He shook his head.

"She said there was blood." The older boy swallowed hard. "The lady came running out, yelling there was blood."

"I went in." Steve rubbed his eyes. "I thought maybe she fell, hit her head, or . . . But she wasn't in there."

"There was blood," Will said again.

"Your mom wasn't in there," Steve said firmly. "She's somewhere else."

"Where?" Pete demanded in a voice perilously close to weeping. "Where did she go?"

"That's what we're going to find out." Peabody spoke with easy confidence. "Pete, Will, why don't you help me get drinks for everybody? Inspector Warren, is it okay if we forage in here?"

"You bet. I'll give you a hand." He added a warm smile. "And make it Jake."

Eve slid into the booth. "I need to ask you some questions."

"It was too much blood," he said in a soft voice, a voice that wouldn't carry to his children. "A fatal loss of blood. I'm a doctor. I'm an ER doctor, and that much blood loss without immediate medical attention . . . For God's sake, what happened to Carolee?"

"Do you know her blood type, Dr Grogan?"

"Yes, of course. She's O Positive."

"You're certain?"

"Yes, I'm certain. She and Pete are O Positive. I'm A Positive, so's Will."

"It wasn't her blood. The blood in the restroom wasn't hers."

"Not hers." He trembled, and she watched him struggle for composure, but his eyes teared. "Not her blood. Not Carolee's blood."

"Why were you going to Staten Island?"

"What? We weren't. I mean . . ." He pressed his hands to his face again, breathed, then lowered them. Steady nerves, Eve thought. She imagined an ER doc needed them. "We were taking the ride over, then we were going to ride back. Just for the experience. We're on vacation. It's our second day on vacation."

"Does she know anyone in New York?"

"No." He shook his head slowly. "She wasn't in there. But she wouldn't have left Pete. It doesn't make sense. She doesn't answer her 'link. I've tried it over and over." He pushed his across the table. "She doesn't answer."

He glanced toward the concession where Peabody and Jake kept the kids busy, then leaned closer to Eve. "She would never have left our boy, not willingly. Something happened in that room. Somebody died in that room. If she saw what happened —"

"Let's not get ahead of ourselves. We're still searching. I'm going to check on the status."

Rising, she signaled to Peabody. "It's not her blood. It's the wrong type."

"That's something. They're really nice kids. They're scared."

"They're on vacation. Don't know anyone in New York according to the husband, and he comes off straight to me. What doesn't come off is how a body could disappear, a woman who we'll presume for the moment is alive could disappear, and potentially a killer/abductor could disappear. They're here somewhere. Get the wit statement, though I don't think that's going to add anything. I'm calling in more officers, ours and DOT's. We're going to need to get data, statements and do a search on every person on this damn ferry before we let anyone off."

"I'll take care of our end before I talk to the woman. Ah, he's kind of flirting with me."

"What? Who?"

"The adorable inspector."

"Please."

"No, seriously. I am spoken for," Peabody added with a flutter of lashes, "but it's still flattering to have cute guys flirt."

"Do the job, Peabody."

Shaking her head as her partner went out to do just that, Eve gestured to Jake. "We're going to need more men. I can't let anyone off until we've confirmed IDs, interviewed and searched."

"Over three thousand people?" He let out a low whistle. "You're going to have a revolt."

"What I've got is a missing woman, and very likely a dead body somewhere on this vessel. I've also got a killer. I want somebody in here with them," she added. "I want a look at all security discs, cams, monitors."

"That's no problem."

"We need an e-man to try to triangulate the signal with Grogan's 'link. If she's still got it, we may be able to locate her. What time did she go missing?"

"As close as we can determine, right about one thirty."

Eve glanced at her wrist unit. "More than an hour now. I want to —"

She heard the boom, the gunfire crackle, the shouts. Before the next blast, she was rushing through the door and out on deck.

Passengers whistled, stomped, cheered, as an impressive shower of color exploded into the sky.

"Fireworks? For Christ's sake. It's still daylight."

"There's nothing scheduled," Jake told her.

"Diversion," she muttered, and began to push and shove her way in the opposite direction of the show. "Get somebody to find the source, stop it."

"I'm already on it," Jake said and shouted into his communicator. "Where are we going?"

"The scene of the crime."

"What? I can't hear a freaking thing. Say again," he yelled into his communicator. "Say again."

Eve broke through the celebrating crowd, ducked under the barricade.

She stopped as she saw the woman arguing frantically with the DOT officer guarding the door of the restroom.

"Carolee!" she called out, and the woman whirled. Her face was deathly pale with high spots of color on the cheeks, and a purpling knot on her forehead.

"What? What is this? I can't find my boy. I can't find my son."

The eyes were wrong, Eve thought. A little glassy, a little shocky. "It's okay. I know where he is. I'll take you to him."

"He's okay? You . . . Who are you?"

"Lieutenant Dallas." Eve watched Carolee's eyes as she took out her badge. "I'm the police."

"Okay. Okay. He's a good boy, but he knows better than this. He was supposed to wait right here. I'm sorry to be so much trouble."

"Where did you go, Carolee?"

"I just . . ." She trailed off. "I went into the restroom. Didn't I? I'm sorry. I have a headache. I was so worried about Pete. Wait, just wait until I —" She stepped into the snack bar when Eve opened the door. Then slapped her hands on her hips.

"Peter James Grogan! You are in so much trouble."

The boy, his brother, his father, moved like one unit, bolting across the room. "Didn't I specifically tell you not to —"

This time the words were knocked back as her three boys grabbed her in frantic embraces. "Well, for heaven's sake. If you think that's going to soften me up after you disobeyed me, it's not. Or only a little." She stroked the boy's hair as he clung to her legs. "Steve? Steve? You're shaking. What is it? What's wrong?"

He pulled back to kiss her, her mouth, her cheeks. "You — you're hurt. You've hit your head."

"I . . ." She lifted her fingers to touch the bump. "Ouch. How did I do that? I don't feel quite right."

"Sit down. Pete, Will, let your mother have some room. Sit down here, Carolee, let me take a look at you."

When she had, he took her hands, pressed them to his lips. "Everything's okay now. It's okay now."

But it wasn't, Eve thought, not for everyone.

Someone was dead. Someone had caused that death.

They were both missing.

CHAPTER
THREE

"Inspector, I need you to locate the source of those explosives, then I want that area secured. I want a complete list of DOT and ferry employees, including any independent contractors, aboard at this time. I want those security discs. When NYPSD officers arrive, they will support those assignments. Peabody, make that happen. Now."

She glanced toward the Grogan family. She could give their reunion one more minute. "There are lifeboats, emergency evacuation devices on this boat?"

"Sure."

"They need to be checked, and they need to be guarded. If any have been used, I need to know. Immediately. I want to talk to the guard Mrs Grogan talked to when she . . . came back. For now, get his statement."

"No problem. Lieutenant, we're going to have to deal with getting these people, at least some of these people, off."

"I'm working on it. Explosives, employees, discs, emergency evac, secured areas. Let's get on it."

She turned away, moved to where Carolee still sat surrounded by her family.

"Mrs Grogan, I need to speak with you."

"I'd like to treat her head wound." Steve kept his arm protectively around his wife. "And check her out more thoroughly. If there's a medical kit, I could use it."

"I'll find one," Peabody told him, then glanced at Eve. "Our guys will be on board in a couple of minutes."

"Okay. Find the kit. Organize the team. I want another search, every square inch of this ferry. I want the sweepers in that bathroom. I want it scoured. See if you can find out if anyone else has been reported missing."

"Yes, sir."

As Peabody left, Carolee shook her head. "I'm sorry, I'm a little confused. Who are you again?"

"Lieutenant Dallas, NYPSD."

"The police," Carolee said slowly. "You need to talk to me? I know I got a little upset with the security man, but I was worried about Pete. I couldn't find my boy."

"Understood. Mrs —"

"If you're police, do you have a zapper?" Obviously content now that his mother was where she belonged, Pete gave Eve a curious squint.

"Don't interrupt," Carolee admonished.

"Mrs Grogan," Eve began again, but lifted her jacket aside to reveal her sidearm — and the boy flashed her a grin. "Can you tell me what happened, after you and your son went to use the restrooms?"

"Actually, we were going to get drinks, then Pete needed to go, so we swung over that way. I told him to wait, to stay right there if he got out before I did."

"But, Mom —"

"We'll talk about *that* later," she said in a tone that warned of lecture, and the kid slumped down in his seat.

"And then," Eve prompted.

"Then, I waited a minute, watched Pete go in, and I . . ."

Her face went blank for a moment. "That's funny." She offered a puzzled smile. "I'm not quite sure. I must've hit my head. Maybe I slipped?"

"Inside the bathroom?"

"I — It's silly, but I just don't remember."

"Don't remember hitting your head, or going into the bathroom?"

"Either," she admitted. "I must've really knocked it." She tapped her fingers to the bump, winced. "I could use a blocker."

"I don't want to give you anything until I check you out a little more," Steve told her.

"You're the doctor."

Eve thought of a case, not so long before, where memories had been lost. Or stolen. "How bad's the headache?"

"Between crappy and lousy."

"If you try to remember, does the pain increase?"

"Remember hitting it?" Carolee closed her eyes, squeezed them in concentration. "No. It stays between crappy and lousy."

"Any nausea, baby, or blurred vision?" Steve shined a penlight in her eyes to check pupil reaction.

130

"No. I feel like I walked into a wall or something and smacked my head. That's it."

"There was an Out of Order sign on the door," Eve reminded her.

"There . . . That's right!" Carolee's eyes brightened. "I do remember that. So I . . . but I wouldn't — I *know* I didn't go off to one of the other restrooms. I wouldn't leave Pete. I must've gone in. I must've, because I had to come out again, right? He wasn't there waiting. I must've slipped and hit my head, and I'm just a little shaky on the details. I'm not sure I understand why it matters to the police."

"Mrs Grogan, you were missing for over an hour."

"Me? Missing? That's crazy. I just —" But she glanced at her wrist unit, and went sheet white. "But that can't be. That can't be the right time. We were only gone for a few minutes. The ferry ride takes less than a half hour, and we'd barely started. This can't be right."

"Nobody could find you. We couldn't find you," Steve said. "We were so scared."

"Well, God." She stared at her husband, shoved a hand through her hair as it started to sink in. "Did I wander off? Hit my head and wander off? Maybe I have a concussion. I wandered off." She looked down at Pete. "And then I yelled at you when I was the one. I'm sorry, kiddo. Really."

"We thought you were dead 'cause there was the blood." The boy pressed his face to Carolee's breast and started to cry.

"Blood?"

"Mrs Grogan, the DOT officials notified the NYPSD not only because you were, apparently, missing, but because the facilities they believed you entered had a considerable amount of blood on the floor, as well as spatter on the walls and doors of the stalls."

"But . . ." Her breathing went shallow as Carolee stared at Eve. "It's not mine. I'm okay."

"It's not yours. You went into the bathroom," Eve prompted, "despite the Out of Order sign."

"I can't remember. It's just blank. Like it's been erased. I remember watching Pete go into the boys' room, and I . . . I remember seeing the sign, but then, I can't. I would've gone in," she murmured. "Yes, that's what I would've done, just to check, because it was right there and why not look? I couldn't leave Pete. But I don't remember going in, or . . . coming out. But I couldn't have gone in, or I would've come out. Probably screaming if I saw blood all over the place. It doesn't make sense."

"No," Eve agreed, "it doesn't."

"I didn't hurt anyone. I wouldn't."

"I don't think you hurt anyone."

"An hour. I lost an hour. How can that be?"

"Have you ever lost time before?"

"No. Never. I mean, I've lost track of time, you know? But this is different."

"Will, how about getting your mom a drink?" Steve sent his older son an easy smile. "I bet she's a little dehydrated."

"Actually —" Carolee laughed a little weakly. "I could really use the restroom."

"Okay." Eve watched Peabody come back in with a med kit. "Just a second." She walked over to waylay her partner. "Go ahead and give the kit to Grogan, and take the woman to the John. Stick with her."

"Sure. We're on board, and we've got a deck-by-deck search going. I have to say, the natives are getting a little restless."

"Right. They'll have to hang on a little longer."

"I wonder if maybe this whole thing isn't some stupid prank. Somebody dumps a bunch of blood in that bathroom, hangs the sign, sits back and waits for somebody to go in."

"Then why hang the sign?"

"Okay, a flaw in the scenario, but —"

"And how did they transport a couple quarts of human blood? And where did Mrs Grogan go for an hour?"

"Several flaws."

"Stick with her," Eve repeated. "Get their New York address. Let's arrange for them to be taken back so she can get a full check at a health center, and I want a watch on them." She glanced back. "If she saw something, someone, maybe whoever's responsible for the blood will start to worry about her."

"I'll make sure she's covered. Nice family," Peabody added, studying the group.

"Yeah. Welcome to New York."

Eve tracked down Jake.

"All emergency evac devices are accounted for." He passed her a file of security discs. "Those are from all cams on board. The list of employees, DOT officials, is labeled."

"Good. Where the hell did those fireworks come from?"

"Well." He scratched his head. "It looks like they were set off starboard side, probably the stern. That's from figuring the basic trajectory from witnesses. But we haven't got any physical evidence. No ash, no mechanism. Nothing so far, so I'm not sure they were set off from the boat."

"Hmm." Eve pondered and glanced out at the wide harbor.

"The NYPSD is crawling all over the place, and your CI team's covering the crime scene. If it is one," he added. "We've accounted for every DOT employee on board, and between your people and mine, we've been interviewing passengers, concentrating on those who are in the areas of the scene. So far, none of them saw anything. And you have to admit, hauling a body around would attract some attention."

"You'd think."

"What do we do now?"

As far as Eve could determine, there were two options. The killer — if indeed a murder had taken place — had somehow gotten off the ferry. Or the killer still needed to get off.

"Looks like we're going to Staten Island. Here's how we'll handle it."

★   ★   ★

It was going to take time, and a great deal of patience, but nearly four thousand passengers would be ID'd, searched and questioned before they were allowed to disembark at St. George terminal. Fortunately a good chunk of that number was kids. Eve didn't think — though kids were strange and often violent entities to her mind — that the pool of blood was the work of some maniac toddler.

"It's actually moving along okay," Peabody reported, and got a grunt from Eve.

"The search is ongoing," Peabody continued. "So far, no weapon, no body, no evil killer hiding in a storage closet."

Eve continued to review the security disc on boarding on her PPC. "The body's dumped by now."

"How?"

"I don't know how, but it's dumped or transported. Two searches, and this one with corpse detectors. He, or an accomplice, used the fireworks as a distraction. Get everyone's attention in one direction, do what you need to do in the other. Has to be."

"It doesn't explain how he got the DB out of the bathroom."

"No."

"Well, if it wasn't a prank, maybe it's a vortex."

Eve shifted her gaze up, gave Peabody a five-second pitiable stare.

"Free-Ager here, remember. I grew up on vortexes. It's a better theory than abracadabra." On a sigh,

135

Peabody studied the bright, tropical fish swimming behind the glass of an enormous aquarium.

"He didn't toss the body overboard, then dive in and swim away," Peabody pointed out. "Like a fish." Noting Eve's considering expression, Peabody threw up her hands. "Come on, Dallas. There's no way out of the bathroom, not without walking in front of dozens and dozens of people."

"In back mostly, since they'd be looking out at the water. If the blood currently being rushed to the lab proves to have come from a warm body — one we hope to identify through DNA matching — there has to be a way out and a way off, because he used it."

"Parallel universe. There are some scientific theories that support the possibility."

"The same ones, I bet, that support sparkly winged fairies skipping around the woods."

"A mocker." Peabody wagged a finger. "That's what you are, Dallas. A mocker."

"In my world, we call it sane."

Jake joined them. "We're about halfway through. Maybe a little more."

"Find any vortexes, parallel universes or sparkly winged fairies?" Eve asked him.

"Mocker," Peabody repeated.

"Ah . . . not so far." He offered them both a go-cup of coffee. "No weapons, no blood, no dead body either, and so far everyone who's gone through the ticker and the interview station is alive."

"I'm going back on board," Eve told him. "If we get a hit — any kind of hit — contact me. Peabody, with me."

"Hey." Jake tapped Peabody's arm when she started to move off with Eve. "We're probably going to put in a long one here. Maybe we could get a drink after we're clear. You know, decompress."

Flustered, she felt heat rise to her cheeks that was a giddy mix of pleasure and embarrassment. "Oh, well. Um. That's nice — it's nice, I mean, to ask and all that. I live with somebody. A guy. An e-guy. We're . . . you know. Together."

"Lucky him," Jake said, and had her blush deepening. "Maybe, sometime, we can grab a brew, just on the friendly side."

"Sure. Maybe. Ah . . ." She flashed a smile, then shot off after Eve.

"Did you forget what 'with' means?"

"No. In fact, I remembered exactly, in that I'm *with* McNab. I remembered even when Jake hit on me."

"Oh, that's different." Eve shot out a sunny smile that had Peabody's stomach curdling. "Let me apologize for interrupting. Maybe the two of you want to take a break, go get a drink, get to know each other better. We can always puzzle out whether or not we have a missing DB and killer later. We wouldn't want a potential murder investigation to get in the way of a potential romance, would we?"

"I speak sarcasm fluently. He did ask me out for a drink though."

"Should I note that in my memo book, on today's date?"

"Jeez." Sulk warred with smug as Peabody boarded the ferry with Eve. "I'm just saying. Plus I get double credits. First I get the satisfaction credit of being hit on by the sexy DOT inspector, and second I get loyal and true credit for turning him down because I have my personal sexy nerd. I hardly ever get hit on, unless you count McNab — which really doesn't since we cohab — so it *is* noteworthy."

"Fine, so noted. Can we move on?"

"I should get at least five minutes of *woo*. Okay," she mumbled under Eve's withering stare. "I'll put the rest of the *woo* time on my account."

With a shake of her head, Eve crossed the deck, now empty but for cops and sweepers, to speak to a crime scene investigator.

"Schuman, what've you got?"

She knew him to be a hard-bitten, seen-it-all type, as comfortable in the lab as on scene. He'd shed his protective suit and booties and stood unfolding a piece of gum from its wrapper. "What we've got is about two quarts of blood and body fluids, plenty of spatter. Got some flesh and fibers, and a virtual shit load of prints. We're gonna want to get it in for a full workup and analysis, but with the on-scene exam, we got your blood type — A Neg, and spot samples indicate it's all from the same person. Whoever that is would be dead as my uncle Bob, whose demise went unlamented by all who knew him."

He popped the gum, chewed for a thoughtful moment. "I can tell you what we ain't got. That would be a body or a blood trail, or at this point one freaking notion how said body got the hell out of that John." He smiled. "It's interesting."

"How soon can you tell me if the blood came out of a warm body, or came out of a damn bucket?"

"We'll look at that. Wouldn't be as fun, but the bucket'd make more sense. Problem being, the spatter's consistent with on-scene injuries." Obviously intrigued, he chewed and smiled. "Looks like a damn slasher vid in there. Whoever walked in living got sliced and diced, stuck and gutted. Then, you gotta say it's interesting, went *poof*!"

"Interesting," Eve repeated. "Is it clear to go in?"

"All swept. Help yourself."

He went in with her where a couple of sweepers examined the sinks, the pipes.

"We're looking at everything," he told Eve. "But you'd have to have a magic shrinking pill to get out of here through the plumbing. We're gonna take the vents, the floors, walls, ceilings."

She tipped her face up, studied the ceiling herself. "The killer would have had to transport himself, the body, and a grown woman. Maybe more than one killer."

She shifted to study the spatter on the stalls, the walls. "The vic standing about there. Killer slices her throat first; that's what I'd do. She can't call out. We get that major spatter from the jugular wound, partially blocked by the killer's body."

Eve turned, slapped her hand to her throat. "She grabs her throat, the blood pumps through her fingers, more spatter there, but she doesn't go down, not yet. She falls toward the wall — we get the smears of blood — tries to turn around, more smears. He cuts her again, so we have the spatter on the next stall there, and lower on the wall here, so he probably stuck her, and she stumbled back this way." Eve eased back. "Maybe tries to make it to the door, but he's on her. Slice and dice, and down she goes. Bleeds out where she falls."

"We'll run it, like I said, but that's how I read it."

"He'd be covered in blood."

"If he washed up at any of the sinks," Schuman put in, "he didn't leave any trace, not in the bowls, not in the traps."

"Protective clothes? Gloves?" Peabody suggested.

"Maybe. Probably. But if he can get a DB out of here, I guess he could walk out covered in blood. No trail," Eve repeated. "No drag marks. Even if he just hauled it up and carried it out, there'd be a blood trail. He had to wrap it up. If we go with protective gear and a body bag or something along the line, he planned it out, came prepared, and he damn well had an exit plan. Carolee was a variable, but he didn't have too much trouble there either. He dealt with it."

"But he didn't kill her. He didn't really hurt her," Peabody pointed out.

"Yeah." That point was something Eve had puzzled over. "And he could have, easily enough. The door doesn't lock. Safety regs outlaw locks on public restroom doors with multiple stalls. He makes do with a sign, even though this had to take several minutes. The kill, the clean-up, the transport. And Carolee was missing for over an hour, so wherever he went, wherever he took her, he needed time."

"A lot of places on this boat. Vents, infrastructure, storage. You got big-ass ducts for heating and cooling the inside cabin deals," Schuman told her. "You got your sanitary tanks, your equipment storage, maintenance areas. We're going through here, but it doesn't show how the hell he got out of this room."

"So, let's find out where he went and work backward. And we need to find out who the vic was, and why she got sliced on the Staten Island Ferry. It had to be specific, or Carolee Grogan's blood would be all over this room, too."

For the moment, Eve thought, the best she could do was leave it to the sweepers.

CHAPTER
FOUR

"Why didn't he kill Carolee?" Peabody wondered when they were back on deck. "It would've been easier. Just cut her throat, and get back to business. It wasn't as if he worried about covering up a crime. All the blood was a pretty big clue one had been committed."

Eve walked toward the stern, trying to reconstruct a scene that made no sense. "I'm looking forward to asking him. I don't think it's just his good luck she can't remember. Let's see what the medical exam concludes after she's done there. But the bigger question is, yeah, why bother to suppress her memory? And why would the killer have something on him that could?"

"Hypnosis?"

"I'm not ruling it out." She leaned back against the rail, looked up at the twin smokestacks. "They're not real. They're show. Just to keep the ferry looking old-timey. Big. Way big enough for somebody to hide a body and an unconscious woman."

"Sure, if he had sparkly fairy wings and an invisibility shield."

Eve had to laugh. "Point. Regardless, let's make sure they get checked out." She turned when Jake walked toward them.

"We let the last of the passengers through the ticker. Two short. We've accounted for everyone, passengers, crew, concession. Two people who got on didn't get off."

"They just got off before we made port," Eve corrected. "This ferry is out of service until further notice. It's sealed by order of the NYPSD. Guards on twenty-four/seven. Crime Scene hasn't finished, and will continue until they've covered every inch, including those," she added, pointing at the smokestacks.

Jake lifted his gaze to follow the gesture. "Well. That should be fun."

"Something this size, with this layout? There are places to hide, to conceal. He had to know the boat, the layout, at least to some extent."

"Having a place to hide doesn't explain getting out of that bathroom without anyone seeing him. Unless he has the cloak of invisibility."

Jake's remark got a quick laugh from Peabody and a cool stare from Eve.

"We work the wit and the evidence. We'll be in touch, Inspector."

"You're leaving?"

"We'll be following up with the security discs, Carolee Grogan, and the lab. The sooner we identify the victim, if a victim there is, the sooner we can move on the killer. You may want some of your men backing up mine on guard duty. I don't want anyone on that ferry without authorization."

"All right."

"Let's move, Peabody."

"Ah, Detective? Should your situation change . . ."

Peabody felt the heat rise to her cheeks again. "It isn't likely to, but thanks." She scrambled to keep up with Eve's long strides. "He hit on me again."

"I'll mark it down, first chance."

"It's markable," Peabody mumbled. "Really." She risked a look over her shoulder before they boarded the turbo. "I figured we'd be staying, going over the boat again."

"We have enough people on that." Eve braced herself as the turbo shot across the water. "Here's a question — or a few. Why kill in a public restroom on a ferry in the middle of the water? No easy way off. Why not leave the body? Why, if interrupted by a bystander, spare that bystander's life? And go to the trouble, apparently, to secret her away for an hour?"

"Okay, but even if we find the answer to any of the whys, we don't answer the hows."

"Next column. How was the victim selected? How was the method of killing selected? How was Carolee Grogan moved from the crime scene to another location? And straddling columns, why doesn't she remember? How was the body — if there was one — removed? All of it comes back to one question. Who was the victim? That's the center. The rest rays out from there."

"The victim's probably female. Or the killer. One of them, at least, is probably female. It makes more sense, given the location of the murder."

"Agreed, and the computer agrees. I ran probability. Mid-eighties for female vic or killer." She pulled out her 'link when it signaled, saw Roarke's personal code on the readout. "Hey."

"Hey back." His face — that fallen-angel beauty — filled the screen as dark brows lifted over bold blue eyes. "You're out in the harbor? The ferry incident?"

"Shit. How much has leaked?"

"Not a great deal. Certainly nothing that speaks of murder." His voice, Irish whispering through, cruised over the words as she rocketed back toward Manhattan. "Who's dead, then?"

"That's a question. I'm hoping the lab can tell me. I'm heading there, and depending on the answer, I might be late getting home."

"As it happens I'm downtown, and was hoping to ask my wife out to dinner. Why don't I meet you at the lab, then depending on the answer you get, we'll go from there?"

She couldn't think of a reason against it, and in fact, calculated the opportunity to run it all by him. A fresh perspective might give her some new angles. "Okay. It'll be handy to have you right there if I have to bribe Dickhead to push on the ID."

"Always happy to bribe local officials. I'll see you soon."

"It's nice, isn't it?" Peabody asked when Eve stuck her 'link back in her pocket. "Having a guy."

Eve started to shrug it off, then decided the turbo pilot couldn't hear them. Besides, there was no reason not to take a few minutes for nonsense. "It doesn't suck."

"It really doesn't. Having a really cute guy like Jake flirt with me has some frost, but knowing I'm going to be snuggled up with McNab tonight? That's the ice."

"Why do you always have to put you and McNab and sex in my head? It brings pain no blocker can cure."

"Snuggling isn't sex. It's before or after sex. I especially like the after-sex snuggle when you're all warm and loose like a couple of sleepy puppies." She cocked her head. "I'm getting horny."

"So glad you shared that with me. Let's try to get this pesky investigation out of the way so you can go get your puppy snuggles."

"You know, I've got this new outfit I've been saving for a night when —"

"Do not go there. Do not," Eve warned. "I swear by all that's holy, I'll chuck you overboard, then order the turbo to run over you while you sputter in the water."

"Harsh. Anyway, maybe that's what the killers did, just chucked the victim in the water, then jumped in after the body wearing SCUBA gear."

"If he was going to chuck the body in, why move it in the first place? He didn't just want the kill, he wanted the body."

"Ewww. I know, a police detective's not supposed to say 'ewww'. But why would he want the body?"

"A trophy." Eve narrowed her eyes.

"I'm not saying 'ewww'."

"You're thinking it. Proof," she added, "which strikes me as more likely than trophy. A body's unassailable proof of death. Which, at this point, we don't have. He does. Which brings us to another why. Why would he need proof?"

"Payment?" At Eve's nod, Peabody lifted her hands. "But for a hit, it was messy and complicated. It doesn't smell like a pro."

"No, it doesn't. Unless you add in the rest. Missing body, public arena, two people vanishing like smoke. That strikes me as very professional."

It kept her mind occupied on the drive to the lab. And at least she was navigating on solid ground instead of water. New York appeared to have burst open for summer, and out of its nooks and crannies poured tourists and the street thieves who depended on them. Glida carts did brisk business with cold drinks and ice pops, while portable knock-off vendors raked it in with cheap souvenirs, wrist units that might function until the buyer got back to his hotel, colorful "silk" scarves, fashion shades and handbags that could be mistaken for their designer counterparts if you were a half block away and had one eye closed.

But it also brought out the sidewalk florists with their bounty of color and scent and the alfresco diners taking in the sun over glasses of wine or thimbles of espresso.

It added to the street and air traffic, jammed the glides and sidewalks, and yet, Eve thought, it all rushed and roared exactly as it was meant to.

She spotted Roarke before she parked, standing outside the drab edifice that housed the busy hive of the lab and forensics. The dark charcoal suit fit the lean length of him perfectly, and showed a subtle flare with a tie nearly as bold a blue as his eyes.

Black hair fell in a mane around that striking face, shades shielded those stunning eyes as he slipped the PPC he'd been working on into a pocket and started toward her.

She thought he looked like some elegantly urban vid star with just a hint of edge. And she supposed it suited him as one of the wealthiest and most powerful men in the world — and on its satellites — who'd pulled himself by hook or — haha — crook out of the grime of the Dublin alleyways.

"Check on Carolee," she told Peabody. "See if they've finished the medical, have any results."

She watched Roarke's lips curve as they walked toward each other. She didn't need to see his eyes to know they mirrored that smile. And her heart gave a quick, giddy jump. She had to admit Peabody was right. It was nice to have a guy.

"Lieutenant." He took her hand and, though she lowered her eyebrows to discourage him, bent to brush those curved lips lightly over hers. "Hello, Peabody. You look fetchingly windblown."

"Yeah." She brushed ineffectually at her hair. "Boat ride."

"So I hear."

"Check on the wit, Peabody," Eve repeated as she led the way inside.

"What was witnessed?" Roarke wondered.

"Tell me what the media's saying. I haven't bothered to tune in."

"I caught bits and pieces on my way downtown to my meeting, then a bit more after. A woman apparently lost on the ferry, then found. Or not, depending on the report. A possibility someone was injured or fell overboard."

He continued as Eve led them through the maze, signed and badged them through security.

"The main thrust seems to be that DOT and NYPSD officials held up the ferry for over two hours, then additional time with a security search of passengers as they disembarked. A few of the passengers sent various media outlets some vids or statements. So, you can imagine, it's all over the board."

"Fine." Eve opted for a down glide rather than an elevator. "Better that way."

"Is someone missing? Or dead?"

"Someone was missing, but now she's not. Someone might be dead, but there's no body. Passenger count is off by two on disembarking."

"Which might equal victim and killer. How'd they get off the ferry?"

"That's another question." She stepped off the glide. "First, I've got a couple quarts of blood in a public restroom on the ferry. I need to find out who it belonged to."

CHAPTER
FIVE

She wound through the labyrinth bisected by glass walls. Behind them techs worked with scopes and holos, forensic droids, tiny vials and mysterious solutions.

The air hummed in a blend of machine and human into a single voice Eve found just slightly creepy. She would never understand how people worked, day after day, in a vast space without a single window.

She found the chief lab tech, Dick Berenski, sliding his stool soundlessly along his long white counter as he commanded various comps. Dickhead was an irritant, a pebble in the shoe on a personal level, but she couldn't deny his almost preternatural skill with evidence.

He looked up, cocking his egg-shaped head as she approached, and she didn't miss the light in his eyes when he recognized Roarke.

"Got yourself an entourage today, Dallas."

"Don't think about trying to hit up the civilian for liquor, tickets to sporting events or cash."

"Hey." Dickhead couldn't quite pull off offended.

"Let's talk blood."

"Got enough of it. I got the initial sample a couple hours ago, and they're bringing in the rest. We'll run tests on samples of that, too. Could be more than one source. Got my blood guy reconstructing the scene, pool and spatter, from the record. That's a fucking beaucoup of blood."

"Fresh or frozen?"

He honked out a little laugh. "Fresh." He tapped some keys and had squiggles and swirls in bold reds, yellows, blues, filling a comp screen. "No indication the sample had been stored, cold-boxed, flash-frozen, thawed or rehydrated."

He tapped again, brought up another screen of shapes and colors. "Coagulation rate and temp says it hit the air about two hours — maybe a little more — before I tested it. That's consistent with the time it took to get here."

"Concluding the sample came out of a live human, and came out of said human between one and two this afternoon."

"What I said. A Neg, human blood, healthy platelets, cholesterol, no STD. We filtered out trace portions of other body fluid and flesh. Double X chromosomes."

"Female."

"You bet. We'll keep separating other body fluids when we have the larger samples, and the sweepers tell me they've got some hair in there. We'll be able to tell you pretty much everything. Fluids, flesh and hair." He grinned widely. "I could freaking rebuild her with samples like that."

"Nice thought. DNA?"

"I'm running it through. Takes some time, and there's no guarantee she's on the grid. Might get a relative. I programmed for full match and blood relations."

Thorough, Eve thought. When Dickhead got his weird little teeth into something, he was thorough. "There were fibers."

"Like I said, we'll separate and filter. I'll give hair and fiber to Harpo. She's the queen. But I can't pull the vic's ID out of my ass. She's either on the grid or — Hey!" He swiveled, scooted as the far comp beeped. "Son of a bitch, we got a match. I am so freaking good."

Eve came around the counter to study the ID photo and data herself. "Copy to my unit," she ordered. "And I want a printout. Dana Buckley, age forty-one, born in Sioux City, why are you dead?"

"Nice-looking skirt," Berenski commented, and Eve ignored him.

Blue-eyed blonde, she thought, pale skin, pretty in a corn-fed sort of way. Five-six, a hundred thirty-eight, parents deceased, no sibs, no offspring, no marriage or cohab on record. "Current employment, freelance consultant. What does this personal data tell us smart investigators, Detective?"

"That the deceased has no family ties, no employer to verify identification or give further data on said deceased. Which makes a smart investigator go *hmmm*."

"It does indeed. She lists a home and office address here in New York. Park Avenue. Peabody, run this down."

"It's the Waldorf," Roarke said from behind her.

152

"As in Astoria?" Eve glanced back, caught his nod, and the look in his eyes when they met hers.

She thought, Crap, but said nothing. Not yet.

"Check and see if they have her registered," she told Peabody. "And get a copy of the ID print, show it to the desk staff to see if they make her. Quick work, Berenski."

"After quick work, I like to relax with a good bottle or two of wine."

She took the printout and walked away without a second glance.

"Worth the shot," Berenski said at her back.

"There's nobody by the name of Dana Buckley registered at the Waldorf," Peabody told her as she caught up to Eve. "No make from the desk staff. This new data rates a second *hmmm*."

"Go back to Central, do a full run on her. You can start on the security discs. Send copies to my home unit. I'm going to swing by, reinterview Carolee, show her the printout. Maybe she'll remember seeing the vic."

"We were lucky to get a DNA match that fast. I'll tag you if I dig up anything on her." She sent a quick smile to Roarke. "See you later."

Eve waited until she and Roarke were in her vehicle, with her taking the wheel. "You knew her."

"Not really. Of her, certainly. It's complicated."

"Is there any way you could be connected to this?"

"No. That is, I have no connection to her."

Eve felt the knot in her stomach begin to loosen. "How do you know her, or of her?"

"I first heard of her some years ago. We were working on a prototype for some — at the time — new holo technology. It was very nearly stolen, or would have been if we hadn't implemented multiple layers of security. As it was, she got through several before the red flag."

"Corporate and/or technological espionage."

"Yes. I didn't know her as Dana Buckley, but as Catherine Delauter. I expect you'll find any number of IDs before you're done."

"Who does she work for?"

He lifted a shoulder in a dismissive if elegant shrug. "The highest bidder. She thought I might be interested in her services, and arranged to meet me. That's seven or eight years ago."

"Did you hire her?"

He glanced at Eve with mild exasperation. "Why would I? I don't need to steal — and if I did, I could do it myself, after all. I wasn't interested in her services, and made it plain. Not only because I don't — never did — steal ideas. It's low and common."

Eve shook her head. "Your moral compass continues to baffle me."

"As yours does me. Aren't we a pair? But I warned her off not only for that, but because she was known — and my own research confirmed — not only as a spy but an assassin."

Eve glanced over quickly before she pushed through traffic. "A corporate assassin?"

"That would depend on the highest bidder, from what I learned. She's for hire, or apparently was, and didn't quibble at getting her hands bloody. Peabody won't find any of this in her run. A large percentage of her work, if rumor holds, has been for various governments. The pay's quite good, particularly if you don't mind a bit of throat slitting."

"A techno spy, heavy into wet work, takes a ride on the ferry. And ends up not just dead, but missing. A competitor? Another kill for hire? It struck me as a pro job, even — maybe because — it was so damn messy and complicated. It's going to get buckets of media when the rest of the data leaks. Who would want that?"

"A point proven?" He shrugged again. "I couldn't say. Was the body dumped off the ferry?"

"I don't think so." She filled him in as she wound and bullied her way to the East Side. "So, as far as I can tell, he moved the body and the wit, in full view of dozens, maybe hundreds of people. And nobody saw anything. The wit doesn't remember anything."

"I'll have to ask the obvious. You're sure there were no escape routes in the room?"

"Unless we've got a killer who can shrink to rat size and slither down a pipe, we didn't find any. Maybe he popped into a vortex."

Roarke turned, grinned. "Really?"

Eve waved it away. "Peabody's Free-Agey suggestion. Hell, maybe he waved his magic wand and said, 'Hocus-pocus'. What?" she said when Roarke frowned.

"Something . . . in the back of my mind. Let me think about it."

"Before you think too hard?" She veered into the health center's lot. "Just let me point out there is no magic wand, or rabbit in the hat, or alternate reality."

"Well, in this reality, most people notice when a dead body's paraded around under their noses."

"Maybe it didn't look like one. They have a couple of maintenance hampers on board. The killer dumps the body in, wheels it out like it's just business as usual. And no, we haven't found any missing hampers, or any trace in the couple on board. But it's a logical angle."

"True enough." Once she'd parked, he got out of the car with her. "Then again, logic would say don't kill in a room with only one out, and a public one, don't take the body, and don't leave a witness. So, it may be hard to hold to one logical line when the others are badly frayed."

"They're only frayed logic until you find the reason and motive." Eve pulled out her badge as they walked into the health center.

The Grogans crowded into a tiny little room with Carolee sitting up in bed, a bouquet of cheerful flowers in her lap. She looked tired, Eve thought, and showed both strain and resignation when she saw Eve come in.

"Lieutenant. I've been poked and prodded, screened and scanned and scoped. All over a bump on the head. I know something bad happened, something awful, but it really doesn't have anything to do with me."

"You still don't remember anything?"

"No. Obviously I hit my head, and I must've been dazed for a while." Her hand snuck from under the flowers to reach for her husband's. "I'm fine now,

156

really. I feel fine now. I don't want the boys to spend their vacation in a hospital room."

"It's just a few hours," Steve assured her. The youngest, whose name was Pete, Eve remembered, crawled onto the bed to sit at his mother's side.

"Still. I'm sorry someone was hurt. Someone must've been hurt, from what Steve said. I wish I could help, I really do. But I don't know anything."

"How's the head?"

"It pounds a little."

"I have a photo I'd like to show you." Eve offered the printout of Dana Buckley. "Do you recognize her? Someone you might've seen on the ferry."

"I don't think . . ." She lifted her hand to worry at the bandage on her forehead. "I don't think . . ."

"There were a lot of people." Steve angled his head to look at the photo. "We were looking out at the water most of the time." He glanced with concern toward the monitor as his wife's pulse rate jumped. "Okay, honey, take it easy."

"I don't remember. It scares me. Why does it scare me?"

"Don't look at it anymore." Will snatched the photo away. "Don't look at it, Mom. Don't scare her anymore." He thrust the photo back at Eve. "She was in the picture."

"Sorry?"

"The lady. Here." He pulled a camera out of his pocket. "We took pictures. Dad let me take some. She's in the picture." He turned the camera on, scrolled back through the frames. "We took a lot. I looked through them when they had Mom away for tests. She's in the picture. See?"

Eve took the camera and looked at a crowd shot, poorly cropped, with Dana Buckley sitting on a bench sipping from a go-cup. With a briefcase in her lap.

"Yeah, I see. I need to keep this for a while, okay? I'll get it back to you."

"You can keep it, I don't care. Just don't scare my mom."

"I don't want to scare your mother. That's not why I'm here," Eve said, directly to Carolee.

"I know. I know. She — that's the one who was hurt?"

"Yes. It upsets you to see her photo."

"Terrifies me. I don't know why. There's a light," she said after a hesitation.

"A light?"

"A bright flash. White flash. After I see her picture, and I'm scared, so scared. There's a white flash, and I can't see anything. Blind, for a minute. I . . . It sounds crazy. I'm not crazy."

"Shh." Pete began to stroke her hair. "Shh."

"I'm going to speak to the doctor. If Carolee's clear, I want to get her and our boys back to the hotel. Away from this. We'll get room service." Steve winked over at Will. "In-room movies."

"God, yes," Carolee breathed. "I'll feel better once we're out of here."

"Let's go find the doctor," Eve suggested and sent a glance at Roarke. He nodded, and moved to the foot of the bed as Steve went out with Eve.

"So, Mrs Grogan, where would you be staying here in New York?"

It took another thirty minutes, but Roarke asked no questions until they were out of the health center. "And so, how is the lady?"

"I had the doctor dumb it down for me. He was giving it to the husband — he's a doctor, too — in fancier terms."

"You can keep it dumbed down for me."

"She's good," Eve told him, "no serious or lasting damage. The contusion, mild concussion, and most interestingly what he dumbed down to a 'smudge' on her optic nerves — both eyes. He seemed to be pushing for another test, but he'd already done a recheck and as the smudge was already dissipating, I don't think Steve's going to go for it. Added to it, the brain scan showed something wonky in the memory section — a blip, but that's resolved, too, on retest. Her tox is clear," Eve added as she got back into the car. "No trace of anything, which is too damn bad, as that's where logic was leading me."

"A memory suppressor would've been logical. And may be yet." He shook his head at her look. "We'll have some things to check into when we get home. You'll likely have to follow up with the Grogans?"

"Yeah."

"Then you'll find them at the Palace. They'll be moving there tonight."

"Your hotel?"

"It seems they're a bit squeezed into a room at the moment, and it struck me they could use a bit of an upgrade for their troubles. Plus the security's better there. Considerably."

"I'm putting a watch on them," Eve began, then shrugged. "It is better." She engaged the 'link to update her men on the change. "Let's go home and start 'checking into'."

CHAPTER
SIX

Summerset, Roarke's man about everything, wasn't lurking in the grand foyer when Eve walked in. She spied the fat cat, Galahad, perched on the newel post like a furry gargoyle. He blinked his bicolored eyes twice, then leaped down with a thud to saunter over and rub against her legs.

"Where's Mr Macabre?" Eve asked as she scratched the cat between the ears.

"Stop." Roarke didn't bother to sigh. The pinching and poking between his wife and his surrogate father were not likely to end anytime soon. "Summerset's setting things up in my private office. We need to use the unregistered equipment," he continued when she frowned. "Any serious digging on your victim is going to send up flags to certain parties. And there's more."

He took her hand to lead her up the steps.

"If I don't dig into the vic through proper channels, it's going to look very strange."

"You have Peabody on that," he reminded her. "And you can do some of your own, for form. But you won't find what you're after through legitimate channels. Set up your runs, on Buckley, the Grogans, the possible causes of this optic smudge. All the things you'd routinely do. Then come up and meet me."

He lifted her hand to kiss her fingers. "And we'll do the real excavating. She's a freelance spy and assassin, Eve, who works for the highest bidder or on a whim. That work would definitely include certain areas of the U.S. government. You won't get far your way."

"What's the 'more'?" She *hated* the cloak-and-dagger crap. "You said there's more?"

But he shook his head. "Start your runs. We'll go over what I've heard, know, suspect."

Since there was no point in wasting time, Eve walked into her home office to set up the multiple runs and searches. She sent an e-mail to Dr Mira, the NYPSD's top profiler and psychiatrist, to ask about the validity of mass hypnosis. It made her feel foolish, but she wanted a solid opinion from a source she respected.

Before compiling and updating her notes, she checked in with Peabody, and read over all the initial lab and sweepers' reports. No witnesses had come forward to claim they'd seen anything unusual, including any individual transporting a dead body. Which was too bad, she mused. Also in the too-bad department was the report that the pipes and vents within the crime scene were just too damn small to have served as an escape route.

Solid walls, no windows, one door, she decided. And that meant, however improbably, both killer and victim had exited through the door.

He hadn't stepped into Peabody's vortex, hadn't employed an alien transporter beam or flourished a magic wand. He'd used the damn door. She just had to figure out how.

She made her way to Roarke's private office, used the palm pad and voice recognition to enter. He sat behind the U-shaped console with the jewel-toned buttons and controls winking over the slick black surface. The privacy screens shielded the windows and let the evening sunlight filter into the room in a pale gold wash. A small table stood by those windows, set with silver domed plates, an open bottle of wine, the sparkle of crystal.

His idea of a working dinner, she mused.

He'd already tied his hair back — serious work mode — and commanded keyboard and touch screens with rapid movements.

"What are you hacking into?" she asked.

"Various agencies. CIA, Homeland Security, Interpol, MI5, Global, EuroCom, and that sort."

"Is that all?" She pressed her fingers to her eyes. "I was going to stick with coffee, but now I think I need a drink."

"Pour me one. And after I get these to auto-search, I'll tell you a story over dinner."

She poured two, pleased the wine was red, which lowered the chances of something healthy like fish with steamed vegetables on the plates. She peeked under the silver cover and was instantly cheered. "Hey, lasagna!" Then, on closer study. "What's this green stuff in there?"

"Good for you."

"Why is good for you mostly green? Why can't they make it taste like candy or at least pizza?"

"I'm going to get my R and D right on that. And we're going to speak of R and D, as it happens. There now." He sat back, nodded at his screens. "We'll see what we see." He rose, crossed to her. Taking up his glass, he tapped it to hers, then smiled. "I think I'll have another of these," he decided, and cupped her chin before taking her mouth with his.

"No distracting with wine and lip-locks," she ordered. "I want to get to the bottom of this. The whole thing is . . . irritating."

"I imagine it is, to someone of your logical bent." He gestured for her to sit, then settled across from her. "Your victim," he began, "was a dangerous woman. Not in an admirable way. Not like you, for instance. She fought for nothing, stood for nothing, save her own gain."

"You said you didn't really know her."

"This is what I know of her. It's not the first time I've looked into her, which will make tonight's work a bit easier on that score. Information on her is, naturally, sketchy, but I believe she was born in Albania, the result of a liaison between her American mother and an unknown father. Her mother served in the U.S. Diplomatic Corps. She traveled with her mother extensively, saw and learned quite a bit of the world. It seems she was recruited, at a young age, by a covert group, World Intelligence Network."

"WIN?"

"Which was exactly their goal. To win data, funds, territories, political positions — however it was most expedient. They only lasted a decade. But in that decade, they trained her, and as she apparently showed considerable ability and no particular conscience, used her in their Black Moon sector."

"Wet work."

"Yes." He broke a hunk of bread in two, passed her a share. "Somewhere along the line, she opted to freelance. It's more lucrative, and she'd have seen WIN was fragmenting. She tends to take high-dollar jobs, private or government. As I said, I had a brush with her several years ago. I believe, two years after that, she killed three of my people in an attempt to acquire the data and research to new fusion fuel we had under development."

Eve ate slowly. "Did she target you? Have you been a target?"

"No. It's generally believed I'm more useful alive than dead, even to competitors or . . . interested parties. I'm able to fund the R and D, the science, the manufacturing, and others may hope to steal it. Nothing to steal if you cut off the head."

"That's a comfort."

He reached across for her hand. "I watch out for myself, Lieutenant. Now, depending on the source, your victim is given credit, so to speak, for anywhere from fifty to two hundred and fifty deaths. Some were in the game, some were just in the way."

"You couldn't find her." Eve watched him as she ate. "You thought she killed three of your people, so you'd have tried."

"No, I couldn't find her. She went under, considerably under. I thought she might be dead, having failed to secure what she was hired for." He studied the wine in his glass. "Apparently I was wrong."

"Until now. It's unlikely she was on that ferry to sight-see."

"Very. It might've been a meet or a target, but odds are it was business."

"Double-cross. But someone like this, experienced, how does she get caught off guard and taken out? Someone she knew? Someone she trusted or underestimated maybe? Another spook? Another assassin?" She felt the frustration rising again, like flood water behind a dam. "Why so freaking public?"

"I couldn't begin to guess. Tell me what you think about this smudge, this flash of light."

She blew out a breath. "I left a message for Mira, asking her about the possibility of mass hypnosis. And that sounds crazy when I hear myself say it out loud. Not as crazy as vortexes or invisibility cloaks, but in that mix of nuts. Still, we've dealt with mind manipulation before. The tiny burn in the cortex found in autopsy after suicides, manipulated by your pal Reeanna Ott."

"Hardly my pal, as it turned out." But he nodded to show they were on the same page. "Manipulation, in that case, done through audio."

"So, a possible manipulation done optically," Eve finished. "One that affects memory. But it has to do more. I can almost swallow people wouldn't remember seeing someone haul out a dead body, but I have to figure they wouldn't just let him by in the first place. And Carolee, whether she was conscious or unconscious, her kid wouldn't have just stood where he was, would he, if he saw her come out? So, maybe we're dealing with a device that can manipulate behavior, or sight, and memory? That's a big jump. Mass hypnosis suddenly doesn't sound so crazy."

"There have been rumors, underground and through the tech world, of a device in development. A kind of stunner."

"Ah. Got one of those." Eve tapped the weapon at her side she'd yet to take off.

"Not your conventional stunner, but one that renders the target incapacitated through an optical signal rather than the nervous system. It sends a signal, through light, that shuts down certain basic functions. Essentially, in a theory not that far from your mass hypnosis, it puts the target into a kind of trance. Hocus-pocus." He lifted his wine glass in half salute. "It's often referred to as that, which made me think of it when you used the term. The rumors are largely dismissed, but not entirely."

"We're talking dozens of people," Eve argued. "Potentially hundreds."

"And the idea this device exists, and has a possibility for that sort of range, is . . . fascinating. And used as a weapon? Devastating."

Eve pushed up from the table to pace. "I hate this kind of shit. Why can't it just be regular bad guy crap? You've got money, I want it, I kill you. You've been screwing my wife, it pisses me off, I cut out your heart.

No, I've got to worry about disappearing bodies and weapons designed to turn the lights out on masses of people. Crap."

"It's an ever-changing world," Roarke said lightly.

She snorted. "How much credence do you and your R and D people put into this device?"

"Enough to be working on something similar — and a counter-device. Though both are still in the theoretical stages. I'm getting the data for you," he added, gesturing toward the console.

She sat again, drummed her fingers on the table. "Okay, say this device exists, and was used today. Say its existence speaks to why Buckley was on that ferry, either with the device in her possession or with the hopes to make that so. It still doesn't explain why she was murdered in the way she was, or why her body was taken off the ferry. Stealing or obtaining the device, even killing Buckley to get it, that's business. Basically exsanguinating her and taking what's left? That's personal."

"I wouldn't argue, but business and personal often overlap."

"Okay." She lifted her hands and swiped them in the air as if clearing a board. "Why remove the body? Maybe to prove the hit, if it's hired. Maybe because you're a sick fuck. Or maybe to buy time. I like that one because it's weirdly logical. It stalls the identification process. We have to depend on a DNA search and match. And then, we get what appears to be an innocuous vic, corn-fed Iowa-born female consultant. Maybe, given some time, we'd dig under that, have some questions. But the bigger puzzler would remain, at least initially, *how* rather than *who*, since we had the who."

"But, because I wanted to spend a bit more time with my wife, I happened to be there when she was identified."

"Yeah. You recognized her, and that's a variable the killer couldn't have factored in."

"Logical enough," Roarke agreed. "But buy time for what?"

"To get away, to deliver the device and/or the body. To destroy the body, certainly to get the hell away from the scene. This spy stuff doesn't work like the job. It's convoluted, covered with gray areas and underlying motivations. But when you wipe away all of that, you've still got a killer, a victim, a motive. We cross off random, because no possible way. It wasn't impulse."

"Because?" He knew the answer, or thought he did, but he loved watching her work.

"The sign on the door, the getaway. It was vicious — all that spatter. A pro wouldn't have wasted time with that. Cut the throat, skewer the heart, hit the big artery in the thigh. Pick one and move on. But blood doesn't lie, and the spatter clearly says this was slice, hack, rip."

The light softened as they spoke, and he wondered how many couples might sit in the evening light over a meal and talk of blood spatter and exsanguination.

Precious few, he supposed.

"Are you sure none of the blood was the killer's?"

She nodded. It was a good question, she thought, and only one of the reasons she liked bouncing a case around with him. "Reports just in, taking samples of every area of spatter, and several from the pool, confirm it all belonged to Buckley."

"Then she was caught seriously off guard."

"I'll say. So, specific target, specific location and time, personal and professional connections. Add one more element, and I think it matters. Whoever killed Buckley didn't kill Carolee Grogan when it would've been easier, more expedient and even to his or her advantage to do so."

"Leaving her body behind. More confusion," Roarke agreed. "A longer identification time on the blood pool. A killer with a heart?"

She tossed back the rest of her wine. "It's more that a lot of people with a heart kill."

"My cynical darling."

She rolled her eyes. "Let's see what we've got so far." She jerked a thumb toward the console.

Roarke walked back behind the command center, sat. Then, smiling at Eve, patted his knee.

"Please."

"And thank you," he said, grabbing her and tugging her down. "There now, this is cozy."

"It's murder."

"Yes, yes, on a daily basis. Now, see here, we're through several levels on HSO, but then, I've been through that door before." He brushed his lips over her cheek. "And making some progress on the others. They'll have done some code shifting and housekeeping since my last visits, but see there, we're re-routing with them."

170

"I see a bunch of gibberish, numbers and symbols flashing by."

"Exactly. Let's see if we can nudge it along." He reached around her, began tapping keys. "There are all sorts of tricks," he continued as the codes zipped by on the screens. "Realignments, firewalls, fail-safes, trapdoors and backdoors. But we keep updating along with them."

"Why? Seriously, why do you need access to this stuff?"

"Everyone needs a hobby. What we want here are eyes-only personnel files, their black ops consultants. And verification if the device rumored to exist does indeed exist. Eyes-only again, but the trick would be to find where it might be tucked and by whom. Ah well, bugger it. Let's try this way."

Assuming from the oath and his increased tapping that he'd hit a snag, Eve wiggled away. "I'm getting coffee, and I'm going to run some data of my own."

When his answer was a grunt, she knew playtime was over. It was time for serious work.

CHAPTER
SEVEN

Using an auxiliary computer, Eve initiated her own search for any mention of a device such as Roarke had described. She found several articles on medical sites detailing the memory suppressive drugs and tools used during routine surgeries, others edging toward hypnotherapy in both medical studies and gaming.

She also found a scattering of fringe blogs raging about government mind control, enslaving of the masses and the ever-popular doomsday warnings. A nation of human droids, forced experimentation, personality theft and human breeding farms were on their top-ten list of predicted abominations. This led her to others claiming to have been abducted by aliens in league with the shadow forces of government.

"I'm surprised the government has time to, you know, govern, when they're so busy working with aliens and their anal probes or pursuing their mission to turn the global population into mindless sex droids."

"Hmm," Roarke said, "there's government, then there's government."

She glanced over to where he sat, fingers flying, eyes intent. "You don't actually believe this crap? Alien invasions, secret bunkers in Antarctica for experimentation on human guinea pigs."

He flicked his glance up. "Icove."

"That was . . . Okay." Hard to argue when they'd both nearly been killed when dismantling a subversive and illegal human cloning organization. "But aliens?"

"It's a big universe. You should get out in it more often."

"I like one planet just fine."

"In any case, I have your victim. No, don't get up." He waved her back. "I'll put it onscreen. Data, wall screen one. This is from HSO, but the data matches what I've got from the other sources."

"Dana Buckley," Eve read. "With her three most common aliases. Same age as her current ID. But with the biographical data you had."

"Now it lists her assets. The languages she spoke, her e-skill level, the weaponry she was cleared for. Included in her dossier is this list." He scrolled down. "Names, nationalities, ranks if applicable, dates."

"Her hit list," Eve mumbled. "They know or believe she's killed these people, but they let her walk around."

"Undoubtedly she killed some of those people for these agencies. They let her walk around until now because she's useful to them."

Eve dealt with murder every day, yet this offended and disturbed her on some core level she wasn't sure she could articulate.

"That's not how it's supposed to be. You can't just kill or order someone's death because it's expedient. We've managed to virtually outlaw torture and executions; if a cop terminates in the line, he has to go through testing to ensure it was ultimate force that was necessary. But there are still people, supposedly on *our* side, who would use someone like her to do their dirty work."

"People who use someone like her rarely, if ever, get their hands dirty."

"She was a psychopath. Look at her psych profile, for God's sake." Eve swung an arm at the screen. "She should've been put away, just like the person who did her needs to be put away."

He watched her as she read the data onscreen. "You have less gray area than most."

"You think this is acceptable? Jesus, read the list. Some of them are kids."

"Collateral damage, I expect. And no," he added as she swung around, her eyes firing. "I don't think it's acceptable to kill for money, for the thrill or for expedience. There may be more gray in my world than yours when it comes to killing for a cause, but that's not what she did. It was profit and, I believe, for fun. And I suspect, if it had been Buckley standing in that room when Carolee walked in, those boys would be grieving for their mother tonight instead of cuddled up with her watching in-room movies."

"Not all assassins are created equal?" Calmer, she angled her head as she studied the screen. "We need to look at this list, see if we can connect any of these names to someone in the same business. Someone skilled enough to get the drop on her."

174

"I'll set it up. Meanwhile, there's interesting data on the device. This memo was issued two days ago." Again, he ordered the data onscreen.

" 'The Lost delayed. Owl to commence new series of tests in Sector Twelve. Owl request for seventy-two and blackout approved.' " Eve puzzled over it a moment. "She's not Owl. Who'd code-name a female assassin — a young, attractive one — Owl?"

"We can go over the earlier memos, but I'd say Owl would be in charge of the development of the device."

"The Lost. You lose time, yourself, your memory of what happened when you're . . . gone. So, if this Owl or someone under him/her had it, maybe it was an exchange. No, no, it was a set-up. It was planned. He had to have a way off the damn ferry, so none of it was spontaneous. Delayed? But if it was used, it was complete."

"It wouldn't be the first time a member of the team decided to go free agent."

"Fake a delay so you could sell it, but you don't sell it. You walk away with whatever she had in that briefcase and the device. A twofer. If this is the last memo in the file, HSO isn't yet aware they have a problem."

"Still another reason to take the body," Roarke pointed out. "Buys that time you spoke of. Maybe he had another offer. Or wants to renegotiate the fee, from a safe location."

"It wasn't about money," Eve murmured, "not just about money. Buying time, yeah, that plays. She won't be identified, officially, to the media until tomorrow."

"There's more. Photos of some of her work. Images onscreen, slide-show method," he ordered.

She'd seen death, in all its forms, too many times to count. She watched it now, roll over the wall screen. Rent flesh, spilled blood, charred hulks.

"Some of these, of course, were very bad people. Others, very bad people wanted out of the way. It appears she didn't discriminate. She followed the money. Some might argue whoever killed her did the world a favor."

"And what makes him any better than her?" Eve demanded.

He only shrugged, knowing on some points they would never agree. "Some would argue otherwise."

"Yeah, some would. Let's find Owl." She pushed her hands through her hair. "And I have to figure out a logical way to explain how I came by anything we get out of this tonight."

"The ever-popular anonymous source."

"Yeah, that'll fool everybody who knows us."

He initiated a series of searches, then studied her as she stood still watching death scroll by. "It's harder when the victim is abhorrent to you."

Eve shook her head. "I'm not allowed to decide if a murder victim is worth standing for. I stand for them."

He rose, went to her. "But it's harder when that victim has so many victims. So much blood on her hands."

"It's harder," she admitted. "It can't always be an easy choice. It's just the only choice."

176

"For you." He kissed her brow, then cupped her face, lifted it and laid his lips gently, softly, over hers.

When she sighed and leaned into him, he hit the release on her weapon harness.

"Working," she said against his mouth.

"I certainly hope so."

She laughed when he tugged the harness off her shoulders. "No, I've got work."

"Searches will take a while." He circled her, reaching out to press a control on his console. The bed slid out of the panel in the wall.

"And you figure sex will cheer me up?"

"I'm hoping it's a side benefit to cheering me up."

He circled again, then launched them both toward the bed. She hit with a breathless thump, bounced and, what the hell, let herself be pinned under him.

"Rough stuff."

He grinned. "If you like."

He yanked her shirt over her head, let it fly as he lowered his mouth, with a hint of teeth to her breast.

She arched, urging him on. The violence here, so full of heat and hope, helped erase all those images of blood and loss. And helped her remember that no matter how they might differ on an issue, even an ideology, there was, always, love.

And lust.

She could take — a handful of that black silk hair, a ripple of muscle as she dragged at his shirt in turn. She could feel the pound of her heart and his as they rolled over the bed in a battle they would both win.

He made her laugh, made her breath catch. He made her skin shimmer and her blood swim. And when she wrapped around him, found his mouth with hers again, she could taste the flood of love and lust and longing.

So strong, so sweet. Her body moved under his, over his, agile and quick. The hum of the work that would draw them both back drowned under the thrum of his own pulse when his hands swept over her. Curve and angle, soft and firm. Wet and warm.

She arched again, rising up where he drove her, to break, then to gather again. Open for more, for him.

When he filled her, when they rose and fell, rose and fell, to break together, it gave her not only pleasure. It gave her peace.

Curled against him, warm and naked and replete, it occurred to her Peabody had been right again. After-sex snuggles were very, very good.

"You should sleep." He spoke quietly, stroking her back. "It's late, and there's no urgency on this one."

"I don't know. Isn't there?" She thought how lovely it would be to just close her eyes, to drift away with the scent of him all over her. "Closing the case, maybe that's not so urgent on a technical level. But if the killer did have this thing, this weapon, and still has it, ready to sell it to God knows, doesn't that make finding him, stopping him, part of the job, too?"

"Close the case, save the world?"

She tipped up her head until their eyes met. "You said you had people trying to develop this thing. Why?"

"Better you do it before the other one does. Self-preservation."

178

"I get that. It's always going to be that way. Bad guy has a stick, you get a knife. He has a knife, you get a stunner. The ante keeps going up. It's the way it is. So, there have to be rules and laws, and even when the line blurs, we have to be able to know who the good guys are. If I have the chance to find this guy, stop him before he sells this thing, maybe we hold all of it back for another day."

"The comp will signal when we have extrapolated data. Sleep awhile, then we'll see about saving the world."

It sounded reasonable.

The next thing she knew, the comp was beeping and she was springing up in bed — alone.

"What? Morning?"

"Nearly." Roarke stood behind the command center, shirtless, his trousers riding low on his hips. "And your Owl's come out."

"You found him — her?"

"Him," Roarke said as she leaped out of bed. He glanced over, smiled. "Come over here and I'll show you."

"I bet." She snatched at her shirt, her pants.

"Killjoy. Well, at least get us both some coffee."

"Who is he?" she demanded as she dragged on her clothes.

"That depends. He, like his victim, has gone by more than one name. This data claims him as Ivan Draski, age sixty-two, born in the Ukraine. Other data, which on the surface appears just as valid, has him as Javis

Drinkle, age sixty, born in Poland. As Draski, he worked for the Freedom Republic, the underground, at the end of the Urbans, in communications and technological development. He's a scientist."

She brought the coffee, gulping some down as she read the data.

"Recruited by European Watch Network, techno research and development," Eve continued. "A gadget guy."

"An inventor, yes. He makes the toys."

"An inside guy," Eve mused. "Sure there's some field time clocked here, but primarily during the Urbans. It's primarily science during and after that era."

"Nanotech," Roarke began. "Hyperdimensional science, bionics, psionics and so on. He's worked on all this. It looks to me, according to this data, you owe your stunner to his work, among other things. And yet I've never heard of him. They've kept him tightly wrapped for decades."

"Maybe he decided it was time for a raise and some credit." She tried to make sense of it. "So, he's lured away from EWN to HSO nearly twenty years ago. And still, I'm not seeing wet work here. He's a techno geek."

"A brilliant one. No. No black ops or wet work listed. But look there, his wife and daughter were killed twenty years ago in a brutal slaying."

"That's interesting timing," Eve said.

"Isn't it? Officially a home invasion. Unofficially, a fringe wing of EWN who'd targeted him for his knowledge and accessibility to sensitive material."

180

"They eat their own." When he switched to the crime scene photos, Eve hissed out a breath. "Jesus."

"Mutilated, hacked to pieces." Roarke's voice tightened in disgust. "The girl was just twelve. The wife was a low-level agent, hardly more than a clerk. You have higher clearance, I expect."

"The writing on the wall there. Did you translate?"

"The computer recognizes it as Ukrainian for 'traitor' and 'whore'. Neither EWN nor any other official file on the matter claims credit or responsibility for the killings."

"They were on her list. On Buckley's list of hits in HSO's data banks." She called for the computer to run the list on another screen to verify. "They're there, on her list, but no employer assigned. Nobody's taken credit."

"If there's data on that, it's in another area. If there's any more data on this hit, it's been wiped or boxed. Even I can't get at it from here, or certainly not quickly. You'd have to be inside to get at it."

"He's inside; he found it." There was motive, Eve thought. There was the personal. "Why the hell didn't they destroy the file if they continued to use her, and had him on the payroll?"

"Somebody fucked up, I'd say, but at the core HSO is a bureaucracy, and bureaucracies love their paperwork."

"Does he have a fixed address?"

"Right here in New York."

She looked back over her shoulder at him. "That's too fucking easy."

"Upper East Side, in a town house he owns under the name of Frank Plutz."

"Plutz? Seriously?"

"Frank J. Plutz, employed by HSO, who lists him as Supervisor, Tech R and D, U.S. Division, in their official file. Which of course is bollocks. He's a hell of a lot more."

Now Eve studied the ID shot of a middle-aged man with a thinning crop of gray hair, a round face, a bit heavy in the chin, and mild blue eyes who smiled soberly from the wall screen.

"God. He looks harmless."

"He survived the Urban Wars in the underground, has worked for at least two intelligence organizations, neither of which worries overmuch about spilled blood. I'd say appearances are deceiving."

"I need to put a team together and go visit the deceptively harmless Mr Plutz."

"I want to play. And I very much want to meet this man."

"I guess you've earned it."

His eyes gleamed. "If you don't put him in a cage, I wonder what I can offer him to switch to the private sector."

CHAPTER
EIGHT

As taking down a spy wasn't her usual job, Eve opted for a small, tight team. She had two officers in soft clothes stationed at the rear of the trim Upper East Side town house, McNab handling the com along with Roarke in the unmarked van. She, along with Peabody, would take the front.

It struck her as a bit of overkill for one man, but she had to factor in that one man had over forty years of espionage experience, and had managed to slip off a ferry of more than three thousand people with a dead body.

In the van, she cued up the security tape from the transpo station. "There he is, looking harmless. Computer, enhance segment six, thirty percent."

The man currently known as Frank J. Plutz enlarged onscreen as he shuffled his way through the ticker. "Anonymous businessman, complete with what looks like a battered briefcase and a small overnight bag. Slightly overweight, slightly balding, a little saggy in the jowls."

"And this is the guy who sliced up the high-level assassin, then poofed with her." McNab, his sunny hair slicked back in a sleek tail, his earlobes weighted with a half dozen colorful studs each, shook his head. "He looks a little like my uncle Jacko. He's famed in our family for growing enormous turnips."

"He does!" Peabody gave the love of her life a slap on the shoulder. "I met him last Thanksgiving when we went to Scotland. He's adorable."

"Yeah, I'm sure this one's just as adorable as Uncle Jacko. In a 'leaving a big, messy pool of blood behind' sort of way. He got a weapon — we assume — through the scanners without a hitch. Which, unfortunately, isn't as tough as it should be. More important, from my source, he's headed or been involved in the invention and development of all manner of high-tech gadgetry, weaponry and communications in particular."

"Love to meet him," McNab said and got a quick grin from Roarke.

"Right with you."

"Hopefully you geeks can have a real nice chat soon." Eve shifted her gaze to the other monitor. "I'm not seeing any heat source in there."

"That would be because there isn't." Roarke continued the scan of the house. "I've done three scans each on heat, on movement. There's no one in there."

"Takes the fun out of it. Well, we've got the warrant. Let's go, Peabody. McNab, keep your eye on the street. If he comes home, I want to know about it."

"Mind your back, Lieutenant," Roarke said as she climbed out. "They're called spooks for a reason."

"I don't believe in spooks."

"I bet they believe in you." Peabody jumped down beside her.

Scanning the building, Eve pulled out her master as they approached the door. "We go in the way we would if we had a suspect inside. And we clear the area, room by room."

Peabody nodded. "A guy who can disappear could probably beat a heat-and-motion sensor."

Eve only shook her head, then pounded a fist on the door. "This is the police." She used her master to unlock the door, noted the standard security went from locked red to open green. "He's got cams out here. I can't see them, but he's got them. Still, no backups set on the locks, and the palm plate's not activated."

"It's like an invitation."

"We're accepting. We're going in," Eve said to alert the rest of the team.

She pulled her weapon, nodded once to Peabody. They hit the door, Peabody high, Eve low. Swept the short foyer with its iron umbrella stand and coat tree, and the narrow hallway with its frayed blue runner. At Eve's gesture they peeled off, clearing the first floor, moving to the second, then the third.

"We're clear." Eve studied the data and communication equipment, the surveillance and security equipment ranged around the modest third-floor room. "Blue team, take the first floor. Roarke, McNab, we can use you on the third floor."

"Do you think he's coming back?" Peabody wondered.

"It's a lot to leave behind. I guarantee all this is unregistered, calibrated to duck under CompuGuard radar. But no, he's done here. He's finished."

"His wife and kid?" Peabody gestured to the framed photo on the console.

"Yeah." Eve moved over, opened a mini fridge. "Water and power drinks." She hit menu on the AutoChef. "Quick, easy meals." The sort, she thought, she'd have had in her own mini fridge — when she remembered to stock it — before she'd married Roarke. "Sofa, with a pillow, a blanket, wall screen, adjoining John. He spent most of his time up here. The rest of the house, it's just space."

"It all looks so tidy, kind of homey and neat."

Eve made a sound of agreement as she turned into the next room. "VirtualFit. It's a nice unit. He wanted to keep in shape. A weight machine, muscle balls, sparring droid. Female, and at a guess, just about the height and weight of Buckley."

Eve studied the attractive blonde droid currently disengaged and propped in a corner. "He practiced here." She moved across the room, opened the doors on a built-in cabinet. "Wow, toy chest."

"Holy shit." Peabody gaped at the display of weapons. "Not so much like Uncle Jacko after all."

Knives, bats, stunners, blasters, clubs, short swords, guns, throwing discs all gleamed in tidy formation.

"A couple missing," Eve noted, tapping empty holders. "From the shape, he took a couple of knives and a stunner. In one of his carry-ons, on his person."

"This is a lot to leave behind, too," Peabody commented.

"He did what he set out to do. He doesn't need them anymore." She turned as Roarke came in with McNab,

186

and caught the gleam in Roarke's eyes as he crossed toward the weapons chest. "Don't touch."

The faintest line of irritation marred his brow, but he slipped his hands into his pockets. "A nice little collection."

"Don't get any ideas," she muttered under her breath. "It's next door you might be useful." She led the way and heard both Roarke and McNab hum in pleasure as some men would at the sight of a pretty woman.

"Geek heaven," she supposed. "Seal up, then see what you can find on all this. Peabody, let's take the second floor."

"Do you want me to get someone in to take over street surveillance?" McNab asked.

"He's not coming back. He hasn't been back since he took those weapons out of the chest. He doesn't need this place anymore."

"There are still clothes in the closet," Peabody pointed out when they started down. "I saw them when we cleared the bedroom."

"I'll tell you what we won't find. We won't find any of his IDs, any of his emergency cash, any credit cards, passports."

She moved into the bedroom where the decor managed to be spartan in neatness and homey in its fat pillows and frayed fabrics. She opened the closet.

"Three suits — black, gray, brown. See the way they're arranged, spaces between? Probably had three more. Same with the shirts, the spare trousers. He took what he needed." She crouched, picked up a pair of sturdy black shoes, turned them over to reveal the worn-down heels, scuffed soles. "Frugal. Lived carefully, comfortably, but without any excess. I bet the neighbors are going to say what a nice, pleasant man he was. Quiet, but friendly."

"He's got drawer dividers. Cubbies for socks, boxers, undershirts. And yeah," Peabody added, "it looks like several pairs are missing. Second drawer's athletic wear. T-shirts, sweats, gym socks."

"Keep at it. I'll take the second bedroom."

Across the hall in a smaller room fashioned into a kind of den, Eve opened another cabinet. She found wigs, trays of make-up, facial putty, clear boxes holding various styles of facial hair, body forms.

She saw herself reflected, front and back, in the mirror-backed doors.

She began a systematic search of the room, then the bathroom. He'd left plenty behind, she thought. Ordinary pieces of the man. Hairbrush, toothbrush, clothes, book and music discs, a pair of well-tended houseplants.

Everything well used, she thought, well tended. Very clean, ordered without being obsessive.

Food in the AutoChef, slippers by the bed. It all gave the appearance of a home someone would return to shortly. Until you noticed there was nothing important. Nothing that couldn't be easily replaced.

Except the photo over his work area, she mused. But he'd have copies of that. Certainly he'd have copies of that image that drove him. She studied the wigs and other enhancements again.

188

He'd left all this, and the weapons, the electronics. Left what he'd been all these years? she wondered. He'd done what he'd set out to do, so none of it mattered to him now.

Peabody came in. "I found a lock box, open and empty."

"One in here, too."

"And bits of adhesive behind drawers, behind the headboard."

Eve nodded. "Under the bathroom sinks, behind the John. He's a careful guy. I'd say he kept weapons, escape documents, in several places around the house, in case he had to get out fast."

"We're not going to find him, Dallas. He's in the wind. It's what he does."

"What he *did*. I'd say he's finished, so it depends on what he's decided to do next. Check on the first floor, will you?"

Eve went upstairs to find both Roarke and McNab huddled with the electronics. On a quartet of small monitors she saw various spaces of the house — Peabody walking down the steps, her two men searching, an empty kitchen, the street view from the front of the house. Every ten seconds, the image changed to another location.

"Guy covered his ass double," McNab told her. "This place is hot-wired, not a trick missed. Motion, heat, light, weight. He's got bug sensors every fricking where. And check it."

He flipped a switch and a panel slid open in the wall beside her. She peered in, scanned the stairs and the weapon adhered to the wall. "Emergency evac."

"Icy. Plus, he could shut and bolt that door from right here."

"It's blast-proof," Roarke added. "He's got his C and D buried on here, but we're digging it out. I'd have to say it's not as well covered as I'd expect when you consider the rest of the security."

McNab shrugged. "Maybe he figured he didn't have to worry about anyone getting this far in."

"Or he didn't care particularly what they found at this point."

She glanced back up at the photo. "Possibly. It looks like he's finished, and with or without the cloak of invisibility, gone. No reason to stay in New York. He eliminated his target. We dig here, hoping we find some link to where he might go. If we don't find it, we're going to have to contact HSO."

Roarke gave her a long, cool look. "I don't see the value of that."

"It's not a matter of value. It's SOP. He's their operative. If he's gone rabbit or rogue, and has a device that's as dangerous as this one might be, we'll need their resources."

"Give us a moment, would you, Ian?"

McNab glanced over at Roarke, then at Eve. He didn't need a sensor to feel the blips of tension and trouble. "Ah, sure. I'll . . . ah, see if I can give She-Body a hand."

"This is my job," she began as soon as they were alone. "When I report in with what we have here, Whitney's going to order me to contact Homeland and give them what I have."

"You have nothing," he said evenly, "but the nebulous connection of one Frank Plutz, on the word of an 'anonymous source' connecting him to HSO and to Buckley."

"I have him getting on the ferry, and not getting off, which secured the warrant more than the source did. I have what we found here."

"And what have you found here that verifies he's an operative for HSO, or that he targeted and killed Buckley?"

She felt her stomach muscles quiver even as her spine stiffened. "We know he has a potentially dangerous weapon. He may intend to sell that weapon. In the wrong hands —"

"Homeland's aren't the wrong hands?" Roarke demanded. "Can you stand there and tell me they aren't every bit as ruthless and deadly as any foreign bogeyman you can name? After what they did to you? What they allowed to be done to you when you were a child? Standing by, listening, for Christ's sake, while your father beat you and raped you, all in the hopes they could use him to catch a bigger monster?"

The quivering in her gut became a roil. "One has nothing to do with the other."

"Bollocks. You tried to 'work' with them before, not so long ago. And when you found murder and corruption, they tried to ruin you. To kill you."

"I know what they did. Damn it, that wasn't the organization, as much as I despise it, but individuals inside it. Ivan Draski is probably thousands of miles away by now. I can't chase him outside New York. I don't *know* where he might try to sell this thing."

"I'll look into it."

"Roarke —"

"Goddamn it, Eve, you're not going to ask me to stand by a second time. I did what you asked before. I let it go. I let go the ones who'd had a part in letting you be abused and tormented."

Now it was her heart, squeezing inside a fist of tension. "I know what you did for me. I know what it cost you to do it. I'm not going to have a choice. It's national security. For God's sake, Roarke, I don't want to bring them in. I don't want anything to do with them. It makes me sick. But it's not about me, or you, or what happened when I was eight."

"You'll give me twenty-four hours. I'm not asking," he said before she could speak. "Not this time. You'll give me twenty-four hours to track him."

Here was the cold and the ruthless that lurked under the civilized. She knew it, understood it, even accepted it. "I can stall that long. At twenty-four and one minute, I have to turn it over."

"Then I'll be in touch." He started to walk by her, stopped, looked into her eyes. "I'll be sorry if we're at odds on this."

"Me, too."

But when he walked out she knew sorry was sometimes all you could be.

CHAPTER
NINE

When a trail went cold, Eve's rule of thumb was go back to the beginning. For a second time she stood on the deck of the ferry under a blue summer sky.

"According to the security discs, the victim boarded first." Eve studied the route from the transport station to the deck. "He was easily a hundred passengers behind her. Several minutes behind her."

"It doesn't seem like he could've kept her in view," Peabody commented. "And from the recording, it didn't look like he tried to."

"Two likely scenarios. He'd managed to get a tracker on her, or had set up this meet in advance. Since I can't think of any reason he'd take chances or play the odds, my money is he did both."

"We haven't turned up a thing that points to her meeting a third party on Staten Island."

Eve huffed out a breath. "I'd say we haven't turned up a lot of things. Yet." She started up to the second deck. "She went up here. We've got that from the Grogan kid's camera. The ride over takes less than a half hour, so if she had a meet, and if she planned to make an exchange, she wouldn't have waited too long once they left port. The best we can gauge, Carolee went into the restroom less than halfway through the trip. About ten minutes in."

"But since she doesn't remember, and we've got no body to calculate TOD, we don't know if Buckley was already dead when Carolee went in."

"Odds are." Eve stood at the rail, imagining the roll and hum of the ferry, the crowds, the view. "Lots of excitement as people are boarding, right? Crowds, happy tourists off on an adventure. People would be securing their places at the rails, grabbing a snack, taking pictures. If I'm Buckley, I take my position, scope it out."

She took a seat on the bench. "Sitting here, and you can bet she sat here before or she'd never have picked or agreed to the location, she can judge the crowd, the traffic, the timing. If I'm Buckley, I move to the meet location as close as possible to leaving port."

Rising, Eve strolled off in the direction of the restroom. "That's around ten minutes before Grogan went in. Plenty of time for the kill. If Grogan had gone in before the attack, why not let her finish up, get out? If she'd gone in during, she should've been able to call out or get out and raise an alarm. She went down at the dividing point between stalls and sinks. That's where the sweepers found traces of her blood and skin from her head hitting the floor. She'd just turned at the wall. And got an eyeful."

"Do you think Mira can help her remember?"

"I think it's worth a shot. Meanwhile . . ." Eve detoured toward concession. "Before the eyeful, Carolee and the kid —"

"Pete."

"Right. They start toward the concession area, then swing to the restrooms." Eve followed the most logical route. "Stand here, discuss. Wait for me, blah blah. Carolee watches the kid go in, then notices the sign on the door. Debates, then decides to give it a try after all. And after that, doesn't remember. So we reconstruct. Going with the theory the meet was set in advance, and the murder was premeditation, Draski would go in first. It's a women's room; he's a guy."

"Right. Well, he might've slipped in when most people are focused on the view, but the Out of Order sign. He'd be smarter to go in looking like maintenance. A uniform."

"Which he could've slipped into right next door." Eve gestured toward the other restroom. "If we're dealing with premeditated, and a need to hide or transport the body, he'd need means. No one would question a maintenance guy going into an out-of-order bathroom pushing a hamper."

"None of the hampers were missing."

"He had an hour to put it back. He comes out of there" — Eve pointed toward the men's room — "goes in here. Who notices? Apparently nobody. Inside to wait for Buckley."

Eve pushed open the door. "I doubt he wasted much time once she came in."

"No way to lock the door from inside," Peabody began, "and no way to rig it shut because he needed Buckley to get in."

"Yeah, so he wouldn't waste much time. He'd want to make sure she had the payment, she'd want to make sure he had the device. Just business."

The congealed pool of blood, smeared now from several samplings, spoke to the nature of that business. As did the slight scent of chemicals, the faint layer of dust left by the sweepers spoke of the results of that business.

As did the long-bladed knife on the floor.

"Record on," Eve ordered, then, avoiding the blood still on the floor, approached the knife.

"But . . . how the hell did that get here?" Peabody demanded. "We've got the entire ferry covered with guards."

"Freaking invisibility cloak," Eve muttered, "answers that. So the first question is, why is it here?" She studied it where it lay. "Dagger style, about a six-inch blade. It looks like bone. That would explain how he got it through the security scanners. The natural material would pass, and it's likely he had a safe slot in that briefcase he carried on. Some protection against the scanner for shape, weight."

She coated her hands before lifting the knife. "Good weight. Good grip." Testing, she turned, swiped the air. "Good reach. You don't have to get close in. Arm's length plus six. Me, I'd use a wrist trigger. Click, it's in your hand, swipe, slice the throat."

Peabody rubbed her own. "Have you ever thought about going into the assassination game?"

"Killing for business, for profit, that was her line, not his. His was personal. Sure took him long enough though." She judged the spatter, the pool, swiped a second time, circled, jabbed, sliced.

"And now he goes to the trouble to put the weapon in our hand so we can see what and how."

"Bragging maybe."

Eve turned the blade, studied the blood smears. "It doesn't feel like bragging." She took out an evidence bag, sealed the weapon inside, tagged it. Holding it, she glanced toward the door. "If Carolee came in now, she'd see him, see the body as soon as she turned for the stalls. That puts, what, about ten feet between them, with her less than two from the door. What would most people do when they walk in on a murder?"

"Scream and run," Peabody provided. "And she should've made it, or at least gotten close. Plus, if he'd gone after her like that, you'd think he'd have stepped in some of the blood. She could've fainted. Just passed out cold. Smacked her head on the floor."

"Yeah, or he could've stunned her. Dropped her. A low setting. That would give him a little time to figure out how to handle the variable. He's got to get the body out, but he'd have prepped for that. Lined the hamper maybe, a body bag certainly. Load it up — along with the uniform. It had to be stained with blood."

"Then he'd use the memory blaster on Carolee as she came to."

Eve cocked her eyebrows at the term "memory blaster". "When she's under, he tells her she's going to give him a hand. He'd go out first."

"Mojo the people on this sector of the deck. He could do that as he made his way to wherever he wanted to go. It's one frosty toy."

"It's not a toy. It's lethal. If it does what it purports, it strips you of your will. You lose who and what you are." Worse than death to her mind was loss of self. "You're nothing but a droid until the effects wear off." She studied the knife again. "Sticks, stones, knives, guns, blasters, bombs. Somebody's always looking for something a little juicier. This." Through the evidence bag, she hefted the knife again. "It can take your life. This other thing, it takes your mind. I'd rather face the blade."

She glanced at her wrist unit. Roarke's twenty-four hours was down to twenty and counting. No matter what it cost her, she couldn't give him a minute more.

The little bakery with its sunny two-tops and displays of glossy pastries might have seemed an odd place to meet with a weapons runner, but Roarke knew Julian Chamain's proclivities.

He knew, too, that the bakery, run by Chamain's niece, was swept twice daily for listening devices, and the walls and windows shielded against electronic eyes and ears.

What was said there, stayed there.

Chamain, a big man whose wide face and wide belly proclaimed his affection for his niece's culinary skills, shook Roarke's hand warmly, then gestured to the seat across the table.

"It's been some time," Chamain said, with a hint of his native country in the words. "Four, five years now."

"Yes. You look well."

Chamain laughed, a big, basso bark, as he patted his generous belly. "Well fed, indeed. Ah, here, my niece's daughter, Marianna." Chamain gave the young woman a smile as she served coffee and a plate of small pastries. "This is an old friend."

"Pleased to meet you. Only two, Uncle Julian." She wagged her finger. "Mama said. Enjoy," she added to Roarke as she bustled away.

"Try the éclair," Chamain told Roarke. "Simple, but exquisite. So, marriage is good?"

"Very. And your wife, your children?"

"Thriving. I have six grandchildren now. The reward for growing old. You should start a family. Children are a man's truest legacy."

"Eventually." Understanding his role, Roarke sampled an éclair. "You're right. Excellent. It's a pretty space, Julian. Cheerful and well run. Another kind of legacy."

"It pleases me. The tangible, the everyday, a bit of the sweet." Chamain popped a tiny cream puff in his mouth, closed his eyes in pleasure. "The love of a good woman. I think of retiring and enjoying it all more. You keep busy, I hear, but have also retired from some enterprises."

"The love of a good woman," Roarke repeated.

"So, we've both been lucky there. I wonder why you asked to meet me, and share pastries and coffee."

"We were occasionally associates, or friendly competitors. We dealt honestly with each other either

199

way. We were always able to discuss business, and important commodities. I feel we've lost time."

He watched Chamain's eyebrows raise before the man lifted his coffee for a long, slow sip. "Time is a valuable commodity. If it could be bought and sold, the bidding would be very steep. Time wins wars as much as blood. What man wouldn't want his enemy to lose time?"

"If a weapon existed that could cause such a thing, it would be worth a great deal on the market."

"A very great deal. Such a weapon, and the technology to create others like it, would command billions. Blood would be shed as well as fortunes spent to possess it. Dangerous games played."

"How much might you be willing to pay, should such a thing exist?"

Chamain smiled, chose another pastry. "Me, I'm old-fashioned, and close to retirement. If I were younger, I would seek out partners, form alliances and enter the bidding. Perhaps a man of your age, of your position, has considered such a thing."

"No. It isn't a commodity that fits my current interests. In any case, I would think the bidding would be closed at this date."

"The window closes at midnight. Games, *mon ami*, dangerous games." He gave a long sigh. "It makes me wish I were younger, but some games are best watched from the sidelines, especially when the field is bloody."

"I wonder if the people at home are aware of the game, its current status."

"The people at home seem to have misjudged the game, and the players. Short-sighted, you could say, and their ears not as close to the ground as they might be. Women are ruthless creatures, and excellent in business. Persuasive."

Roarke said nothing for a moment. "If I were a betting man, and on the sidelines, I'd be interested to know a key player has been eliminated, and she's no longer on the field."

"Is that so?" Chamain pursed his lips at the information, then nodded. "Ah, well, as I said, a dangerous game. Try a napoleon."

Within the hour, armed with the cryptic pieces Chamain offered, Roarke sat in his private office. Clearly Buckley intended to make an exchange for the device — or more likely to kill the delivery boy and walk away with it. It was greed and arrogance that killed as much as the blade. Had it been self-defense all along, or a set-up for revenge?

That wasn't his problem, but Eve's, he thought. His would be to track down Ivan Draski and the device. She'd keep her word on the twenty-four hours, just as he had kept his in not seeking revenge on the operatives who'd been a part of allowing her to be tormented and raped as a child, who'd allowed that child to wander the streets, broken and dazed, after she'd killed to save herself.

He'd destroyed the data on those men, for her sake. But their names were etched in his mind. So, he began the process of hacking his way through the agency, and to those men. On a secondary search he began the hunt for Ivan Draski, and Lost Time.

Well into his tasks, he glanced at the display of his pocket 'link when it signaled.

"Yes, Ian."

"As promised, I'm tagging you first, and praying Dallas doesn't skin my ass for it."

"I wouldn't worry."

"Not your ass," McNab replied. "I got through the shields and fail-safes. This guy's mega — more mega because it barely shows that he took down some of those shields and fail-safes so somebody with solid skills could get through."

"Is that so?" Roarke commented.

"That's my take. I'm saying I've got serious skills, but it should've taken me a couple days to get through, not a couple hours."

"Which means he wanted the information to be found." Roarke scanned his own data, jumbled the information and the theories together. "Interesting. What did you find?"

"He's got megabytes on this Dana Buckley, a massive file on her, complete with surveillance — eyes and ears. I did a skim, and if half this stuff is true, she was one bad bitch."

"And he was following her, and documenting."

"Keeping tabs for sure, back, it's looking like, around six months. The thing is, the data goes back years and from a variety of sources. But he didn't start to collect it here until about six months ago. A lot of high-level stuff. I probably don't have the security clearance to skim, but, hey, just doing my job. But here's what's really the frost on the ice."

"He's running an auction."

"Shit." Onscreen, McNab's face fell. "Why have I worked my personal motherboard to the bone? But you only got it partly right. *She's* running the auction, which is a hell of a trick, seeing she's dead."

"Ah." Roarke sat back as it fell into place for him. "Yes, that's clever."

"It's running out of a remote location. It bounces all over hell and back, scrambling the signal. I wouldn't've found the source if I wasn't right at ground zero. And, well, gotta be on the straight, if he hadn't left the bread crumbs. Upper East Side address. Swank. When I run it, I get it's owned by Dolores Gregory. That's one of Buckley's aliases."

"So it is. That's good data. Now you'd better call your lieutenant."

CHAPTER
TEN

Using her master, Eve opened the locks and shut down the security on the Upper East Side apartment. "That was too easy," she told Peabody. "Just like the Plutz town house. We go in hot."

She drew her weapon, went through the door for a first sweep.

Quiet, she thought as she worked right and Peabody left. A lot of expensive space filled with expensive things. The wall of windows led to a terrace lofty enough to provide a river view. Inside, rich fabrics showcased gleaming wood, and art dominated the walls. The same held true in the master bedroom where the closet held a forest of clothes.

"Some digs," Peabody commented. "I think some of those paintings are originals. I guess assassins rate a high pay grade."

"It's the opposite of Draski. She lived high, he lived low. Easy to underestimate somebody who lives the quiet life."

"Easy to get cocky," Peabody added, "when you live the high."

"Yeah, it is." Eve gestured to the security pad on the second bedroom doorway. It blinked an open green.

"Boy, that was careless of her."

"Not her. He laid those bread crumbs, he lowered the security. We're exactly where he wants us to be." She pushed open the door, swept it, then bolstered her weapon.

The room was cold, nearly frigid. A way to keep the body as fresh as possible, she thought, as she studied Dana Buckley. He'd arranged the bloody shell of her in a chair angled to face a framed photo of his wife and daughter, and the single rose he'd placed by it.

"Well." Peabody hissed out a breath. "She's not lost anymore."

"Call it in. You'd better go get the field kits."

While she waited, Eve studied the room. Her lair, she thought. She expected they'd find the equipment unregistered, and much of the data on it illegally hacked. Not so different from her killer's, she thought, right down to the photograph.

On the wall screen the current status of the bidding was displayed. Up to four-point-four billion, she mused, with several hours yet to go.

He hadn't taken the body for proof. Not for a trophy, and only in part to gain that time. In the end he'd brought it here so while her greed ran behind her back she would stare sightlessly at the innocents she'd killed.

He'd taken the body, she thought, to pay homage to his family.

"We've got an e-team and sweepers on the way." Peabody opened a field kit, passed Eve the Seal-It.

Eve nodded and thought they'd find nothing he hadn't wanted them to find. "I want all the data found copied. We'll have to turn it over to whatever agency the commander orders, but we'll have backup." She turned to her partner. "I think we've just spearheaded a breakdown on a whole bunch of really bad guys. The sort of thing that leaks to the media."

"I don't know whether to be happy or scared."

"Be satisfied. Now let's do the job and deal with her. Record on."

Roarke sat back, absorbing the data he'd just uncovered. Odd, he thought, the world was a very odd and ironically small place. And the people in it were never completely predictable. He saved and copied the data, slipped the copy into his pocket.

He walked to the house monitor. "Where is Summerset?"

Summerset is in the parlor, main level.

"All right then, a fine place for a chat."

As he came downstairs he heard voices, and the roll of Summerset's amused laughter. It wasn't unprecedented for Summerset to have company in the house, but it certainly wasn't usual.

Curious, he stepped in. Then stopped and shook his head. "Aye, unpredictable."

"Roarke, I'm glad you've come down. I didn't want to disturb you, but I'm happy to introduce you to an old friend. Ivan Draski."

As the man rose, Roarke crossed the room to shake hands with his wife's current quarry.

"Ivan and I worked together in very dark times. He was hardly more than a boy, but made himself indispensable. We haven't seen each other in years, so we've been catching up on old times, and new."

"Really?" Roarke slid his hands into his pocket where the disc bumped up against the gray button he carried for luck, and for love. "How new?"

"We haven't quite caught up to the present." Ivan smiled a little. "I thought that should wait until your wife comes home. I believe she'll have an interest."

"I'll fetch more cups for coffee." Summerset laid a hand briefly on Ivan's shoulder before leaving the room.

"Are you armed?" Roarke asked.

"No." Ivan lifted his arms, inviting a search. "I'm not here to bring harm to anyone."

"Have a seat then, and maybe you should bring Summerset and myself up-to-date."

Ivan sat, and an instant later Galahad jumped into his lap. "He's a nice cat."

"We like him."

"I don't keep pets," Ivan continued as he stroked Galahad's length. "I couldn't handle the idea of having a living thing depending on me again. And droids, well, it's not the same, is it? I don't want to bring trouble into your home, or cause my old friend distress. If it had been anyone but your wife involved in this, I believe I would be somewhere else."

"Why my wife?"

"I'd like to tell her," Ivan said as Summerset came back.

"The lieutenant's come through the gate." He set the cup down to pour.

"This should be interesting," Roarke murmured. He waved off the coffee Summerset offered, deciding he might need both hands.

Eve walked into the house and frowned. It was rare not to find Summerset lurking in the foyer with the cat at his heels. She heard the rattle of china from the parlor, hesitated at the base of the stairs.

Roarke came to the doorway and said her name.

"Good, you're here. We need to talk. The situation's changed."

"Oh, it has, yes."

"We might as well have this out before I —" She broke off at the parlor doorway when she spotted the man she hunted sitting cozily in a chair with her cat on his lap. She drew her weapon. "Son of a bitch."

"Have you lost your mind!" Summerset exploded as she stormed across the room.

"Get out of the way or I'll stun you first."

He stood his ground while shock and fury radiated from him. "I won't have a guest, and a dear friend, threatened in our home."

"Friend?" She flicked a glance toward Roarke, a heated one.

"Don't waste your glares on me. I just got here myself." But he touched a hand to her arm. "You don't need that."

"My prime suspect is sitting in my house, petting my cat, and you're all having coffee? Move aside," she said coldly to Summerset, "or I swear to God —"

Ivan spoke in a language she didn't understand. Summerset turned sharply, stared. His answer was just as unintelligible, and with a tone of incredulity.

"I'm sorry, that's rude." Ivan kept his hands in plain sight. "I've just told my friend that I've killed a woman. He didn't know. I hope there's no trouble for him over this. I hope I can explain. Will you let me explain? Here, in an easy way, with a friend. After, I'll go with you if that's your decision."

Eve skirted around Summerset. She lowered her weapon, but kept it drawn. "What are you doing here?"

"Waiting for you."

"For me?"

"I feel you need an explanation. You need information. I won't try to harm you, any of you. This man?" He gestured to Summerset. "I owe him my life. What belongs to him is sacred to me."

"Brandy, I think." Roarke handed Summerset a snifter he'd filled. "Instead of coffee." And gave another to Ivan.

"Thank you. You're very kind. I killed the woman calling herself Dana Buckley. You know this already, and, I think, some of the how. I read a great deal about you in the night, Lieutenant. You're smart and clever, good at your work. But the why matters, it must, when it's life and death. You know this," he said, searching her face. "I think you believe this."

"She killed your wife and daughter."

His eyes widened in surprise. "You work quickly. They were beautiful and innocent. I didn't protect them. I loved my work in my own homeland." He

209

glanced at Summerset. "The purpose, the challenge, the deep belief in making a difference."

"You were — are — a scientist," Eve interrupted. "I read your file."

"Then you're very good indeed. Did you find the rest?"

"Yes. Just shortly ago," Roarke answered. "I'm very sorry. Homeland wanted to recruit him," he told Eve, "possibly use him as a mole or simply bring him over."

"I was happy where I was. I believed in what I was doing."

"They considered various options," Roarke continued. "Abducting him, torture, abducting his child, discrediting him. The decision was, as time was of some essence, to strip him of his ties, and offer him not only asylum but revenge."

"They sent that woman to murder my wife, my child, to make it seem like my own people had ordered it. They showed me documentation, gave me the name of the assassins, the orders to terminate me and my family. I should have been home, you see, but I had car trouble that delayed me. They'd rigged it, of course, but I believed them. I of all people should have known how these things can be faked, but I was grieving, I was wild with grief, and I believed. I betrayed good men and women because I believed the lie and was happy to take my pound of flesh. And I became one of them. Everything I've done for these twenty years has been on the blood of my wife and child. They killed them to use me."

210

"Why now?" Eve demanded. "Why execute her now, and with such theatrics?"

"Six months ago I found the file. I was searching for some old data, and found it. The man who'd ordered the murders is long dead, so perhaps there was carelessness. Or perhaps someone wanted me to find it. It's a slippery world we live in."

He stroked the cat methodically. "I thought of many ways to kill her." He sighed. "I've been one for the laboratory for a very long time, but I began to train. My body, with weapons. I trained every day, like the old days," he said with a smile for Summerset. "I had purpose again. I found my way with Lost Time. So apt, isn't it? All the time I'd lost. Time she'd cost me, had stolen from my wife, my baby."

"I'm sorry, Ivan." Summerset laid a comforting hand on his friend's arm. "I know what it is to lose a child."

"She was so bright, the light . . . the proof of light after all those dark times. And this woman snuffed her out, for money. If you've read her files, you know what she was."

He paused, sipped brandy, settled himself again. "I formed the plan. I was always good at tactics and strategy, you remember."

"Yes, I remember," Summerset concurred.

"I had to move quickly, to leak the data to her, to paint the picture that I was dissatisfied with my position, my pay, and might be willing to bargain for better."

"You let her make the approach, let her pick the time and the place so she believed she had the advantage."

Now he smiled at Eve. "She wasn't as smart as you. Once, perhaps, but she was arrogant and greedy. She never intended to pay me for the device and the files I'd stolen. She would kill me, have the device and all the records on it, while others competed. She had no allegiance, you see, to any person, agency, any cause. She liked to kill. It's in her psych file."

Eve nodded. "I've read it."

Again his eyes widened before he glanced toward Roarke. "I think you may be better even than the rumors. How I'd enjoy talking with you."

"I've thought the same."

"In my business there's no law, as in yours," Ivan said to Eve. "No police, so to speak, where I could go and say this woman murdered my family. She was paid to do so. It's . . . business, so there's no punishment, no justice. I planned, I researched and I accessed her computers. I'm very good at my work, too. I knew before she arranged the meet what she intended. To take the money, disable or kill me, then —" He gestured to the case beside his chair. "May I?"

"No. She was carrying this," Eve said as she rose to retrieve the case, "when she got on the ferry."

"It's a bomb. Disabled," he said quickly. "It's configured inside the computer. It's rather small, but powerful. It would have done considerable damage to that section of the ferry. There were so many people there. Children. Their lives meant nothing to her. They would be a distraction."

"Like fireworks?"

"Harmless." He smiled again.

212

"Let me have that." Roarke glanced at Summerset, got a nod, as he took the case from Eve. And opened it.

"Wait. Jesus!"

"Disabled," he assured Eve after a glance. "I've seen this system before."

"You know, I think how we came to meet. The location was her choice," Ivan added. "She thought of me as old, harmless, someone who creates gadgets, we'll say, rather than one who would use them. But old skills can come back."

"Six months to refine your skills," Eve said, "and set the trap."

"Maybe there was a cold madness in the planning, in my dedication to it. Even so, I don't regret. I thought to do it quickly. Slit her throat. Put her in the hamper. I'd use the device to get away."

"How?" Eve demanded. "How did you get off the damn ferry?"

"Oh. I had with me a motorized inflatable." He shifted to Roarke as he spoke now, and his face became animated. "It's much smaller than anything used, as yet, in the military or private sectors. Inactivated, it's the size of a toiletry kit you might use for travel. And the motor itself —"

"Okay." Eve cut him off. "I get it."

"Yes, well." Ivan drew in a long breath. "I had thought I'd do what I'd set out to do quickly, then I'd disappear. But I . . . I can't even remember, not clearly, after I looked in her eyes, saw her shock, saw her death. I can't remember. I think I will someday, and it will be very hard."

Tears glinted in his eyes, and his hand trembled slightly as he drank more brandy. "But I looked down at what I'd done. So much blood. The way I'd found my wife and daughter, in so much blood. There was a stunner on the floor. She must have tried to stop me, I'm not sure. I picked it up. Then the woman came in."

"You didn't kill her when you had the chance."

He shot Eve a shocked stare. "No. No, of course not. She'd done nothing. Still, I couldn't let her just . . . It happened so quickly. I used the weapon on her, and she fell. I remember thinking, this is very unfortunate, a very unfortunate turn of events. In the old days, you thought on your feet or died. Or someone else did."

"You used the device on her when she came around, and took her with you," Eve supplied.

"Yes. I told her to hide. You can influence people when they're under. She was to hide until she heard the alarm. I set it on her wrist unit. Then she was to go back where she came from. She wouldn't remember. She looked so frightened when she came in and saw what I'd done. I didn't want her to remember. I saw her with her children when we boarded. A lovely family. I hope she's all right."

"She's fine. Why the fireworks?"

"A good distraction. You'd think I used them to get away, and I'd already be away. And my little girl loved fireworks. You know the rest, I think. You've hacked into my system at home, and into hers. You have a very good e-team."

"Why did you come here?" Eve asked. "You could be thousands of miles away."

214

"To see an old friend." He glanced at Summerset. "Because you were involved."

"What difference does it make who led the investigation?"

"All," he said simply. "It was a kind of sign, a connection I couldn't ignore." He looked at Eve then with both understanding and sorrow. "I know what they did to you. They ignored the cries of a child being brutalized. They killed my child, who must have cried out for me in fear and pain. The same man ordered both. The slaughter of my family, and some years before the sacrifice of a child's body and mind."

He sighed when Eve said nothing. "I couldn't ignore that. It seemed too important. You and Mylia would be of an age now, had she lived. You lived, and you're part of the family of my old friend. How could I ignore that?"

"How did you come by that information?" Eve asked, her voice flat.

"I . . . accessed it when you married. Because of my friend. I couldn't contact you," he said to Summerset. "It might cause you trouble, but I wanted to know your family. So I looked, and I found. I'm sorry for what was done to you. He's dead, the one who ordered the listening post to do nothing to interfere. Years ago," Ivan added. "I don't know if that comforts you. It comforts me because I believe I would have killed him, killed again if he wasn't dead."

"It doesn't matter. It's done."

He nodded. "So is this. There are dirty pockets in the well of the organization. She, this woman, was one of

215

the things that crawled around inside those pockets. But still, I took her life, and it doesn't, as I thought it would, balance the scales. Nothing can. These people shaped our lives, pieces of our lives, without giving us a choice. They took something deeply personal from us. So, when I learned it was you looking for me, I had to come. If I may?"

He held up two fingers, pointed them at his jacket pocket. At her nod, he reached in carefully and slid out what looked like an oversized 'link.

"It's only the casing," he said when both Eve and Roarke lunged for it. "I dismantled and destroyed the rest. And all the data pertaining to it."

Roarke let out a breath. "Well, bugger it."

Ivan laughed, then blinked in surprise at the sound. "It needed to be done, though I admit it was difficult. So much work." He sighed over it. "If I'm arrested, they'll come for me. Or others like them will come. I have knowledge and skill. Your law, your rules, even your diligence won't stop them. I don't say this to save myself," he said gently. "But because I know they'll find a way to make me use my knowledge and skill for them."

"He saved lives, innocent lives, on that ferry," Summerset said. "He's certainly saved others, perhaps scores of others, by destroying that thing."

"That's not why I went there. I went to kill. The lieutenant knows that. The rest is circumstance. I'm content to leave this in her hands. Content to face justice."

"Justice?" Summerset snarled at the word. "How is this justice?" He rose, rounded on Eve. "How can you even consider —"

"Shut it down. Don't," she added to Roarke before he could speak. She paced away to stand at the window and wait for the war inside her to claim a victor.

"I saw her files, as I'm sure you wanted me to when we found her body. She kept reports and photos of her kills like a scrapbook. She's what I work against every day. So is what you did on that ferry."

"Yes," Ivan said quietly. "I know."

"They will come for you, and whatever obstacles I put in their way so you can face justice won't be enough to stop them. I consider this matter out of my jurisdiction, and will certainly be told the same when I contact HSO to report what I've learned up to the time I walked into this house."

She turned back, spoke briskly. "This is an internal HSO matter, involving one of their people and a freelance assassin they have previously employed. It's possible this is a matter of national security, and I'd be derelict in my duty if I didn't report what my investigation has turned up. I'm going to go up to my office, inform my commander of my findings and follow his directive. You'd better say goodbye to your friend," she told Summerset.

She turned to Ivan, his pleasant face and mild eyes. "Disappear. You've probably got an hour, two at the outside, to get lost. Don't come back here."

"Lieutenant," Ivan began, but she turned her back and walked out of the room.

Epilogue

Roarke found her in her office, pacing like a caged cat. "Eve."

"I don't want any damn coffee. I want a damn drink."

"I'll get us both one." He touched the wall panel and chose a bottle of wine from inside. "He was telling the truth. I got deep enough to find considerable data on him, on his work prior to Homeland, on the decision to kill his family and plant evidence that led to his own organization."

He drew the disc from his pocket. "I made you a copy." He handed her the wine, set the disc on her desk. "And he was telling the truth when he said they, or others like them, would come for him. He would have self-terminated before he worked for anyone like them again."

"I know that. I saw that."

"I know a decision like this is difficult for you. Painfully. Just as you know I stand across the line so it wouldn't be difficult for me. I'm sorry."

"It shouldn't be for me to decide. It's not my place, it's not my job. It's why there's a system, and mostly the system works."

"This isn't your system, Eve. These things have their own laws, their own system, and too many of those pockets inside them don't quibble about letting a child be tortured, don't lose sleep over ordering the death of a child to reach the goal of the moment."

She took a long sip. "I can justify it. I can justify what I just did because I know that's true. It's not my system. I can justify it by knowing if Buckley had gotten the upper hand yesterday, Carolee Grogan would be dead, and that kid waiting for his mother outside the door would be blown to pieces along with dozens of others. I can justify it knowing if I arrested him, I would be killing him."

She picked up the disc from her desk, and remembering what he'd once done for her, snapped it in two. "Don't let him come here again."

He shook his head, then framed her face and kissed her. "It takes more than skill and duty to make a good cop, to my way of thinking. It takes an unfailing sense of right and wrong."

"It's a hell of a lot easier when they don't overlap. I have to get my report together and contact the commander. And for God's sake, get that boomer out of the house. I don't care if it is defused."

"I'll take care of it."

Alone, she sat down to organize her notes into a cohesive report. She glanced over when the cat padded in, with Summerset behind him.

"Working," she said briefly, then frowned when he set a plate with an enormous chocolate chip cookie on her desk. "What's this?"

"A cookie, as any fool could see. It'll spoil your dinner, but . . ." He shrugged, started out. He paused at the door without turning around. "He was a hero at a time when the world desperately needed them. He would be dead before the night was over if you'd taken him in. I want you to know that. To know you saved a life today."

She sat back, staring at the empty doorway, when he'd left her. Then she scanned her notes, the report on screen, the photographs of the dead. They were the lost, weren't they? All those lives taken. Maybe, in a way that nudged up against that line between right and wrong, she was standing for the lost.

She had to hope so.

Breaking off a hunk of cookie, she got back to work.